WALLACE'S SINGER

Russell Boyce

Copyright © 2015 Russell Boyce

All rights reserved, including the right to reproduce this book, or portions thereof in any form. No part of this text may be reproduced, transmitted, downloaded, decompiled, reverse engineered, or stored, in any form or introduced into any information storage and retrieval system, in any form or by any means, whether electronic or mechanical without the express written permission of the author.

This is a work of fiction. The persons and events in this book may have representations in history, but this work is entirely the author's creation and should not be construed as historical fact.

ISBN: 978-1-326-19971-5

PublishNation, London
www.publishnation.co.uk

CHAPTER ONE

Margaret Shows the Way

It was not the best start to the day. It was not the best start to any day. It was certainly not the best start to this day, the sixth February 1292.

I had been summoned to see our Abbot, Friar William. On this freezing February morning, the one thing I couldn't expect was warmth. Friar William was a Dominican. As such, he was a mendicant and a preacher. Oh, he preached at us, all right. One of his favourites was, "*Bernadus valles, montes Benedictus amabat, oppida Franciscus, celebres Dominicus urbes.*" He translated it as, "Bernard loved the valleys, Benedict the mountains, Francis the towns, Dominic the populist cities."

Well, if that was the case, what is Dominican Friar William doing here in Brechin, a god-forsaken small village in the North-East of Scotland where the nearest town was Dundee.

As for being a beggar, it's quite easy to own nothing when, at the snap of your fingers, you can get anything you want from the locals – even the poor ones whose fingers couldn't snap as they'd been worked to the bone. He got everything he needed from the parish of Brechin. Perhaps this mendicant was working on mendacity.

But I was telling you about that morning. I got the summons very early. Long before I needed to rise to do the milking. There was enough moonlight reflecting on the snow covering for me to see outside the window. It looked very cold. But you get used to long, cold nights up here. You go to bed in the dark, well-wrapped and pull the hay close to you. You wake up in the dark, still cold and looking forward to breaking the ice to wash. None of us wear our habits to bed. We try to keep them relatively clean and sweat-free. Most of the brothers have white ones and the wool can get very dirty. Mine is black as I'm only a lay brother. While they pray, I do the work.

I pulled on my tunic, decided not to wash and headed for Friar William's cell. Why a cell I don't know. He had his own Palace in amongst the ten other manses which we called the chanonry, where the rest of the canons lived with their servants and families. But no, Friar William chose a cell.

The little light from my tallow candle flickered. I used to like that pig. She always waited for her food, unlike some of the others who used to nuzzle me as I spread out our scraps. I gave her a name. Margaret. I just like the sound of that name.

Down the outside corridor. What could he be wanting? I know the kale I brought in yesterday was a little dirty, but it was frozen and difficult to clean. I know we're short of milk, but there's hardly anything for the cows to eat. What do you expect? I know I haven't been working at my learning, but there's just so many other things to do.

I reached the small wooden door of the Abbot's cell. I had never been in there before. It seemed a little bit like the altar, like approaching a sacred place. As my hand went towards the handle, I paused. He was humming. One of my favourite chants. Surely he isn't angry. Maybe it wasn't the kale or the milk or the education. My knock was greeted by the call, "Come."

"Ah, Brother Alan. Enter. Sit down", said Friar William, "We have much to discuss."

"Thank you, sire"

The room had no chair. There was the bed with the same hay we all used. There was a little desk with a kneeling pad. There was a candle burning on the table. More of Margaret? He's the Abbot. He's entitled to a beeswax candle. So why the smell?

I could see little else. His hand indicated a stone sticking out from the wall. Not very big, not very comfortable. But then I wouldn't need it for too long – hopefully. Wrapping the black wool of my habit in such a way as to provide something of a cushion I sat on it and waited.

"Brother Alan,"

His hands moved from the clasped position to his face. A craggy face. William was probably every bit as old as he looked. I would guess about 50. Yes, he would probably be about 35 years older than me, if I knew the exact year of my birth. His fingers removed some sleep from his eyes.

"You have a talent."

The silence that followed made me reply, "Thank you, sire". So far my talent couldn't be for conversation.

"We want to use that talent. We want to use it in a special way."

CHAPTER TWO

The Preaching

The stone seat below me already started feeling uncomfortable. Where was he heading? What talent? Strength? I suppose I can handle myself physically better than most of the brothers, but look at the family he comes from. Plenty of muscle there.

As he rubbed his eyes, whatever residue that remained on his finger was being transferred to the rope that dangled from his waist.

"You have always been faithful to your vows?"

"Yes, sire". For once my conversational skills were on my side. Don't ask and don't volunteer.

Friar William rose from his bed. I did likewise. "No, no, stay seated."

Why were there no chairs? I pulled as much material as I could to cushion my nether regions – hadn't been too successful the first time - and waited.

"You remember Friar William?", he asked, for the first time gazing straight into my eye. Now this was tricky. This was a subject seldom discussed and when it was it was usually the subject of trouble.

In front of me was Friar William Comyn, a scion of a very strong political family in Scotland. Probably the most powerful family in Scotland. The Friar William that this Friar William was referring to was Friar William de Crachin. He was this Friar William's predecessor. Although dead for about 20 years, his presence hovered over our Abbey. Without going into the long story, he was never really consecrated and shouldn't really have been a Friar and shouldn't really have had the dealings he had with the local populace and shouldn't have fallen out with Rome the way he did and shouldn't…Let's face it, that Friar William just shouldn't.

"Yes, sire. I mean, I know about him. Well, I've heard about him. Or, I've heard some things about him. I mean not all bad."

Why did I choose this moment to gain the skill of talking?

"Brother Alan, we trust that Friar William is with our Lord, following his repentance. It is not for us to be his judges here on earth. If the Good Lord didn't hear his repentance then he is burning in Hell."

"Yes, sire." Don't say another word. After a pause, Friar William continued;

"He was summoned, as were all the Scottish bishops, to the Second Council of Lyons. Unfortunately, he died before he could undertake the journey to France. I was chosen to go in his place. Although it was 18 years ago, I still remember it well. It was a wonderful occasion. The Church gathered from all over. Did you know that it was that Council in Lyons that recognised our Order?"

"Yes, sire".

"Yes, of course. Anyway, while I was there I was very impressed with the church music. I've told you before that that's where I heard about Guido?"

"Yes, sire." And I've told you before about Friar William's preaching. This was a story I'd heard many times before. Hearing it again was not a problem. Hearing it again in the freezing cold with my bum taking on the imprint of the old masons was.

"Guido was a Benedictine. He started out at the monastery of Pomposa but, after some trouble, moved to Arezzo. It was there that he formed a way of writing down music. The monks could learn the chants much quicker. It was based around *ut-re-mi-sa-sol-lah.* Did I tell you where he got that from?"

"Yes, sire."

"He got it from the first syllables of the first six lines of the hymn *Ut queant laxis,* Hymn to St. John the Baptist. Brilliant. His treatise *Micrologus,* written nearly 250 years ago, with his idea of gamut – his scale – has made our plainsong what it is today."

"Yes, sire."

"The point of telling you this story, Brother Alan, is that I've been hearing more news from France. Their singing has changed. It seems to be different, more exciting."

"More exciting?" If I have to engage in more conversation, maybe the two word strategy is a good one. But I was interested. I love singing. I love our choir. Standing with the brothers all making these sounds is almost magical – but hardly exciting.

"So I hear. Well, that's the point, I don't hear. I want you to hear. I want you to go to France, learn the new singing and come back here and teach it to us."

"Me."

"Yes, you, Brother Alan."

"But I'm a lay brother. What about one of the real brothers? I've never been as far as Dundee before, let alone France. I can't talk the way they do. How would I learn? And I've no idea how to get there. It's a bit far to walk." Where had my new two word strategy gone?

"Brother Alan, of all our brothers, you sing the sweetest. You learn the fastest. Your voice can be the strongest. Singing is the greatest of your talents."

"But my work is here. I look after the fields, the animals. That is my real talent."

"Brother Alan, I asked you a few moments ago if you were faithful to your vows. Like a lot of your other answers you replied 'Yes, sire'. One of your vows is obedience to your Abbot. Your Abbot – I, Friar William – am instructing you to go to France, to learn the new music and come back to teach it to us. Now, what do you say?"

"Yes, sire."

CHAPTER THREE

The Road to Dundee

The next few days were spent with me being terrified and Friar William bringing practical answers to problems.

Need a horse? One appeared from a local chieftain. What sins had he confessed? New clothes? No problem. Various new changes appeared. Brother William didn't think I should travel all the way in my habit. And so it went on. Money, letters of introduction, maps. Well, kind of maps. But the real preparation were the people Friar William had invited to our Abbey to give us the intelligence for the journey. Take the maps for instance.

He brought several people to meet me who had recently returned from France. From their experiences it became possible to start marking out the route and consider our sea crossings.

Gradually I moved from terror - to interest - to excitement.

I was given my own horse. She looked something of a cross between a heavy horse and a highland pony. Square and with a good girth, though not massive, she was built for endurance. She also had a good temperament. I could ride, of course, but now I had to get used to a saddle. As we practised, she taught me. I called her Meg.

I was given my own sword. A broadsword. I could use a sword, of course, but now I had to get used to a long one. This one had a handle of almost a foot, with a blade of three and a half feet. As we practised, it taught me nothing. I called it words I wouldn't care to share with you.

But through all this, it was what I was finding out that was interesting. Everyone warned me my journey was dangerous.

Scotland had no King. Our King had died six years ago and wee Margaret – I do like that name – who was going to be our Queen died coming over from Norway. As a result there was some tension between our chiefs. Edward in England was back from France, but his Kingdom was by no means settled. Things weren't much better in France for my journey to Paris. This journey could be dangerous.

From excitement - to interest - to terror.

A route was worked out for me, with places to stay and people to meet. I was warned that these letters of introduction were my assurance of a safe passage. Lose them at my peril.

My first stage was only to Dundee, a two day ride for Meg. A quicker horse could have made the twenty eight mile journey faster, but she had a long journey to make. No need to push her on the first day.

My leaving was something of an occasion. I had no parents to bid me farewell, or girlfriend to wave a white cloth, but a lot of villagers joined the brothers. All the packs had been strapped round Meg but there was just enough room for me to sit on the saddle with my newly acquired skills. I was wearing my habit with a covering black cloak. March is still cold in Scotland. Strapped across my back, diagonally, somewhat incongruously, was my broadsword. I hoped the picture was of a strong, young man, with the trappings of wealth, about to start an adventure. Probably the picture was of a gauche young man, overladen, riding into the unknown.

With waves and accompanying cheers, we set off. I tried to hold my back straight until I was out of sight. It would look more imposing. As I gave a last wave, trying to remember my last view of our Abbey, I turned back to face the future and simply whispered to Meg, “We’re on our own now, girl. Let’s see what this France looks like.”

CHAPTER FOUR

The Alehouse

But before Paris, Dundee.

I was to head for St Mary's Church on the outskirts of the town. There I had to meet one John Blair, who had recently returned from France.

On arrival, I handed over Meg to be fed and stabled to the brother who met me. I also gave him my sword asking him to keep it safe. He told me that Brother John was in the chapter house and pointed me to the eastern wing of the church.

He was. Or, at least, there was a monk sitting by himself at a table. He was nursing a goblet of wine. He looked in his mid-thirties and was dressed in a habit not dissimilar to mine. The Benedictines usually wore black in contrast to our cleric monks who wore white. His hair was tousled and looked as if it hadn't been washed for some time. As was the rather shaggy beard that covered two-thirds of his face. His eyes peered into the distance scarcely acknowledging my presence for some time.

"Aye?" he ventured eventually.

"Brother John? Brother John Blair?", I replied.

"Might be. And ye are?"

"Brother Alan. Brother Alan Murray."

"Frae?"

"I've come from the abbey at Brechin."

"One of Friar William's young men. Whit are you wanting here?"

"I have this letter for you."

He took the letter and as he undid the seal he grunted indicating that I should sit down. I blessed the Benedictines for having a more relaxed attitude to life that extended to chairs. I sat and waited as he read. Like some court magician he reached under his tunic and produced another goblet. Without speaking, he filled it from the jug with wine and pushed it my direction. I might have preferred water but thought it better not to ask. In any case I wasn't sure if the water here was as clean as our water.

He raised his goblet in a kind of toast. I joined him. As we both drank, he threw the parchment to one side.

"Brave little brother. So yer gang tae France?"

I can't remember how it developed but somewhere I had built up a distrust for those who only asked questions. Taking another sip, nay swallow, I replied, "Aye, sir, that is my intention" and, fighting fire with fire, "and you have shortly returned?"

"This wine is crap," he said replenishing both the goblets, "but the water here is pish. Now there's a question for Boniface. Is crap better than pish?"

"Boniface?" I asked.

"Ye should wear that tunic with mair knowledge. Ye'll never get tae wear the white. Boniface is oor leader. Oor wan sent frae God. Oor Pope."

"Oh."

"Oh! Do you Dominicans live in another world?"

"No, I should have known. But, as you can see, I am a lay Brother."

"Oh, Ah can see. Come, lay Brother, journey wi' me into the world of theology. Oor brethren outside these walls need tae be led by those of us who understand the scriptures and can interpret them. Exegesis. Noo, is crap better than pish?" Exegesis

"I don't know."

"Ye don't know. Ye don't know. The Good Lord turned water into wine. Wine is pish ergo pish is better than crap. Theological."

"Maybe I'll just stay a lay Brother."

His laugh could have been heard somewhere down the River Tay. "Drink up. Drink the pish. Ah like you taking the pish. Whit's your name again? Alan?"

"It is, sir."

"Let us finish this jug and go and find some crap, Alan. Ah know an alehouse where they have almost acceptable crap."

With that he poured the last of the contents of the jug into our goblets, and, with one drink, emptied his own goblet. I struggled to finish mine as he was already on his feet wrapping his habit around him.

"Come," he said, "oor drink awaits."

He was through the door and into the street in no time. He pulled his cowl over his head and headed up a street. He kept close to the house walls and with a wave of his hand indicated that I should follow him, keeping also to the shadows. After a few minutes he stopped at a door and knocked in a rhythmical pattern. The door opened enough for him to get through. He grabbed my wrist and pulled me in behind him.

It was dark and musty. The candles, such as there were, offered a very low light. He propelled me onto a bench and headed towards the corner of the room. In the gloom I could just see that he was having two mugs of ale poured. The landlord, if that was what he was, as the place was more of a front room than an alehouse, was a small wizened man whose head never kept still, jerking as if a magpie on the lookout. Brother John brought the tankards over, though I saw no sillar changing hands.

"Here's tae your trip, young Alan. May God go with you."

We drank on with our mugs being refilled several times. Initially our conversation was of pleasantries. Our past lives, our present times. He had been to school here in Dundee. He had also done part of his training in the University of Paris.

Things got more interesting as he discussed the state of Scotland. Too many factions all competing to rule. Too many people wanting to get their hands on the taxes. Too many chiefs forming alliances that might work today but would fail tomorrow.

He talked about Edward Longshanks convening a Council to decide the next King of Scotland that took place last year. I knew that. He complained about how a King of England should be deciding who should be the King of Scotland. I agreed with that. He explained that there were twenty-one contenders for the Scots throne. I didn't know that.

He talked of one contender, John Balliol. It was more than obvious that he didn't approve of him being chosen. He was quite forthright about that. He didn't like how the powerful family of Comyns supported Balliol. I decided to withhold the information that my Friar William belonged to the house of Comyn.

He talked of a William Wallace. They were at school together in Dundee. They were both taught by an uncle of Wallace, another priest. William and he became friends. Both were going to be priests, but Wallace changed his mind. John reckoned he was the one for Scotland, the one to bind the factions.

His speech was becoming a little slurred. He was managing to consume the ale at twice my speed. And then he stopped. He was still, with his eyes staring into the distance, just like they were in the chapter house when I first met him.

"*Dic te verum, libertas optima rerum: Nunquam servili sub nexu vivito,fili",* he intoned.

Then his eyes glanced back into mine and held the gaze.

"I'm sorry. I don't have Latin."

"You don't have Latin? Do ye ha'e French?"

"No."

"Clever. Going to be an interesting journey fur you. Whit Ah said wis, *I tell you truthfully, freedom is the best of all things: Never live under the yoke of slavery, my son.* It was something William and I learned at school. It became a kind of motto o' his. Ye see, we learned Latin and French at school."

"Never live under the yoke of slavery," I repeated.

"Come. Time tae get back. We have managed to miss services, so we should enter quietly."

He rose, grunted towards the landlord whose head twittered more like a sparrow than a magpie, and staggered towards the door. I followed, not knowing if I should offer a supporting hand. He opened the door and we slipped out to a very dark night. No need to look for the shadows now.

Just as we were about to turn a corner, an arm came from a darkened doorway, grabbed John and clubbed him over the head. He collapsed to the ground. The assailant emerged, took one look at me and fled up the vennel. I gave chase.

CHAPTER FIVE

Breakfast at St Mary's

The man ran quickly ahead of me, darting into the small streets and vennels and closes. He lost me. Whichever way I looked, there was no sign of him. Damn. He was tall. He seemed to have a slight limp. His right shoulder drooped. He was memorable.

I made my way back to John. Well, at least, I did eventually. Retracing my steps in these confined quarters wasn't easy and I made a couple of accidental detours.

When I reached him, he was still lying on the ground though by the groans he was coming to. I noticed some people had passed on the other side. No Good Samaritans in Dundee then.

"Are you all right? "I asked.

His hand wiped his head and came off with quite a smear of blood.

"Gie me a haund up," he replied.

With some trouble, he regained his feet. "What was that about?" I asked. "He didn't try to rob you or anything."

"None of your business. Let's get back to St. Mary's afore someone else decides tae jine in the fun."

"I lost him."

"Of course ye did. And just as well ye did."

"Did you know him?"

"How do Ah know? Ah didn't even see him."

"Then why are you saying it's just as well I didn't catch him?"

"Too many questions, Alan. St.Mary's."

He was staggering a bit so I used my arm to give him some support. But as we reached the Church he became more secure in his walking. As we reached the large wooden door of the Church, he pulled his cowl over his head. His hand moved up to pull the ring that worked the bell. Turning to me, he said, "Nothing happened."

"Nothing happened?"

"Nothing happened. Right?"

"Nothing happened."

He said he would see me at breakfast and left me to be shown to my room by the brother who had opened the door.

It was a small cell, but after tonight, and the quantity of ale, it was as welcome as one of the chambers of the rich. I would sleep. I slept.

The ringing of bells and the sound of chanting woke me. My head belonged to someone else, but, unfortunately, my mouth belonged to me. After ablutions, I headed for some food. A Brother slopped some porridge into a bowl and poured some small ale. John was already sitting at table eating his. He had obviously cleaned the wounds on his head and tried to cover the injury with his hair. As I sat down beside him, he shuffled along the bench to give me slightly more room.

"Good Morning," I said, with some attempt to be cheerful.

"Uuuh."

We ate on. Eventually he said, "Ye leaving today?"

"I thought so. Long way to go."

"Whaur ye heading?"

"Going to Stirling. Cross the River Forth there."

"Stirling? Ye don't want to go there."

"Why not?"

"Because the castle's held by a bastard Englishman. Goes by the name of Norman Darcy. There is always the possibility of trouble at Stirling. Look Ah'm heading for Dunfermline. Come wi' me. Ah'll be stopping overnight at the Abbey at Cuilross. Ye can get a boat there to take ye across the river."

"Why not? I'll enjoy the company."

"Unless some fellow attacks me again?" He finished his porridge and took a swallow of the ale.

"Pish. " He moved a little closer and lowered his voice. "Ah'm a man of opinions. Ah'm not afraid to express my opinions. Especially when they're right. It seems to be that not everyone thinks Ah'm right. That was the cause o' last night."

"But… I didn't see much of him, but I would have recognised him if he'd been in the alehouse."

"No, no. He wisnae there. Ma friend the landlord owes me a favour. I sorted out some wedding stuff for his pregnant daughter.

Ma recompense is free ale. Ah guess he has decided that he has provided enough ale by now. Ma reckoning is he sent a messenger to tell some folk that Ah was there so that they could wait tae greet me when Ah left. Ma reckoning is also that they do not quite share ma opinions on who is entitled to rule oor country. Ma reckoning is he's a Comyn's man."

It still didn't seem to be the right time to talk of Friar William. "So Dunfermline?"

"Aye, Dunfermline. Maybe by David's Church Ah'll find some who are intelligent enough to share ma opinions. If not, Ah'll consider joining a silent order. Not ma natural inclination, but safer. You ha'e, of course, a horse?"

"Yes, a good one."

"And arms?"

"I have a broadsword."

"That's fur fighting in battle. It's no use on the road. Ye need something smaller, lighter, deadlier. Ah'll sort it oot. Be ready in an hour. It's time tae get the stour of Dundee aff the soles of ma shoes."

So I prepared for the next part of my journey. I kent not how important it would be.

CHAPTER SIX

Cuilross

When they brought Meg round, she already had a short sword and scabbard strapped to her harness. I mounted her just as John rode into the courtyard.

"Ready?" he asked.

"Aye, John, ready." With that he rode on ahead. There were no brothers to say farewell to him. There were no plans discussed about our journey. There was no conversation for the first couple of hours. He just rode.

We slept in the open on our first night. It was quite warm. July in Scotland can be nice. When we needed food and drink, he would leave me with the horses and approach the door of some dwelling. I'm not sure what was said, or indeed what was offered in return, but he always came back with enough for both of us. Maybe he just got on with common people – if not Comyn people.

When we arrived at the Abbey at Cuilross – pronounced by the monks Coorus – it was already getting dark. We were shown to our cells. Not really much different from Brechin. Dark and damp, with the same smell from the candle that pervaded my own cell up north. Sleep came easily. I was almost as tired as Meg must have been. The only difference was I would be fine in the morning, she would need a couple of days to recover.

Morning began with the first service. These Cistercian monks had different versions of chants, but it didn't take me long to adjust. I hadn't sung since leaving home. It was a pleasure, once I found their cadences, to open up and sing. I drew looks from the other monks, but I could see from the corners of their mouths that their looks were those of pleasure. As the Abbot led us in the last canticle, our voices joined and began to soar. It felt like the stones around us increased the echo in appreciation. The Abbey resounded to the glory of God.

We filed out quietly and were led to where we all should sit. It was so like Brechin. The benches had the same degree of discomfort, the tables showed the same evidence of years of scrubbing and the oatmeal produced the same kind of gruel.

Then a little wooden chalice was passed down the line of the silent, seated monks. Each, with his first finger and thumb, sprinkled some white, shiney grains onto the porridge. I did the same. The signal for eating, as always, was the Abbot lifting his wooden spoon and having his first sup.

It was as if there was an explosion in my mouth. I had never tasted food like this. Each spoonful brought a sensation my tongue had never experienced. The gruel became ambrosia. What magic was this that these monks had?

My bowl was empty long before the rest. I had to sit in silence till the others finished. I didn't mind. I still had the aftertaste buzzing in my mouth. I looked across at John. He too was finishing and I was sure I could detect the beginnings of a smile in the corners of his mouth. And it wasn't my singing that produced it.

As we rose to leave, one of the older monks, who I later found out was Father Ambrose, approached me. He pulled back his cowl and, smiling, said,

"Would you like to see our garden, my son?"

"Yes, Father."

"Come, "he said. "As we are not allowed the sin of pride, our garden is just our larder."

He led me west of the Abbey. To someone who was used to the cattle and the sheep and the oats of Brechin, it was a strange sight. These monks had rows of plants growing. I didn't recognise any of them, but they stood like miniature hedgerows. Different sizes, different leaves, but all in disciplined order.

"If this was my work, I would be proud," I said to Father Ambrose.

"All to the glory of God and giving us ample food," he replied. "Although, while glorifying the Father, I cannot understand why he allows insects to damage our crops. Not much glory in eaten leaves."

He bent down and pulled a little plant out of the soil. I couldn't tell what it was, but it wasn't the same size or in line with the others round about. He walked on and stopped at a more bunched crop. He pulled off a leaf and gave it to me.

"Taste that," he said.

I put it in my mouth and chewed cautiously. Yet another new taste. It was fresh and tart at the same time.

"We call it mint. We use it to make a brew. Not like our ale. We just pour hot water over the leaves."

"It's good," I said, not having the vocabulary to describe taste. "What was the white stuff we just put on our oatmeal?"

He laughed.

"Salt," he replied. "We make it down there by the river. We take it for our health."

"I've never tasted anything like it. It's very good. It's a bit like the sea up at Brechin."

"Yes, it's very good for our health." His eyes were twinkling. "It is to the glory of God that something that is so good for us also tastes so good."

"May the glory of God spread up to Brechin," I replied.

He sat on a bench which faced the river below. There were trees, but the view was magnificent. All the way down to the river and the countryside beyond and the hills.

"Oh but it has, young man, it has."

I suppose my quizzical expression obviated the need for me to put the question into words.

"We haven't heard singing like that in the Abbey for many a year," he continued.

"Oh that," was the best I could manage, quickly adding, "Of course, to the glory of God."

"You have an excellent voice. So pure. Your Abbot must be very proud of you - were pride not a sin."

"He has never said, sir. Though he sent me on this trip to find out about the new singing in France."

"The new singing?"

"Yes. They seemingly sing the same words to different tunes at the same time."

"A metaphor for some of our chieftains."

"Excuse me?" I questioned.

"Never mind. And how does one voice achieve this?"

"No, many voices."

"I see. And you have been sent to learn?"

"Yes."

"Such a long journey. I hope it will be worth it." He paused. I wasn't sure if he was considering the political alliances of our chieftains or the thought of someone journeying to France to learn singing.

Rising he said, "Well, I must work. I just wanted to say that your singing pleased us all this morning. Look." He pointed down to the river. "There's a boat arriving at the harbour. Always a matter of excitement. Why don't you walk down and see what it's bringing – apart from news, that is."

Without waiting for a reply, he rose and took up a long-handled tool and strode off into the garden.

But he was right. I had nothing to do. I might as well investigate the small hamlet by the shore of the River Forth and see what the boat had brought in.

CHAPTER SEVEN

Business at the Harbour

The path down was rough and narrow. Probably just made by the monks going up and down the hill. The hill was steep, very steep. All right for going down if you watched your step, but the way back would be a different matter. The hamlet consisted of only a few houses – stone built with some form of grass roofing. There was an open area near the harbour. More of a jetty really, with wooden piles driven into the river bed and planks of rough hewn wood forming a walkway. Three small boats were tied up.

There was the odd person sitting around. One man was fixing nets, so I took it he was a fisherman. Another was shelling oysters.

I walked towards the boats.

"Hullo, Father."

She had been sitting behind a large rock. I hadn't seen her.

"It's not Father. I'm a lay brother."

"What can I call you then, lay brother?"

"Alan is my name."

"Alan."

"And yours?"

"Margaret, but they call me Meg."

That name again. You can like pigs. You can like horses. But you can really like this Meg. I couldn't see the colour of her hair with her head covering, but her blue eyes suggested it might be fair. Her face was beautifully round, like an apple with its red skin emphasising her cheek bones. She was small, very small. But under the hairy cloth that formed her dress were shapes…

"You live here, Meg?"

"No across there. A place called Faukirk."

She pointed to the other side of the river.

"So what are you doing here?"

"I trade. I bring nails across and sell them to the fishermen and boat builders and I buy salt from the monks to take back."

"I tasted salt this morning. It was good."

"Yes, but very expensive. I can only afford to buy a little each time."

She sat back on the rock which had previously concealed her. There was no room to sit beside her. I looked out to sea. My talent sure wasn't for conversation. Oh, how I wanted to find something to say.

"What are you doing here in Cuilross, Alan?"

It was a simple question and yet she made it seem that my answer really mattered to her.

"I'm on my way to France."

A stupid answer. No reason to be in Cuilross just to be going to France. But my stomach seemed to be echoing the beats of my heart and I was glad to get anything out.

"A long journey. Why France?"

"It's a long story."

"I have the time. Tell me the long story."

I thought of John up at the Abbey, I hadn't told him that I was going down to the harbour. I'm sure he wouldn't care less where I was, but I didn't know when he was leaving for Dunfermline.

"No, I better get back up the hill."

She stood, took my hand and squeezed it. John could wait!

I gave her a truncated version of my story – missing out the events at Dundee. As I talked, we walked along the shoreline. My refound talent for conversation sometimes faltered, but prompted by the occasional 'Go on' from Meg, I finally finished.

"So, here I am in Cuilross."

"And when do you leave?" she asked.

"Probably tomorrow."

"So soon?"

"Well, Meg will be rested and I should get going. It's a long way."

"This Meg won't be rested."

I had told her my story. I just had omitted to tell her the name of my horse.

"Meg is my horse."

There was a slight pause. She looked up at me.

"Do you like riding Meg?"

Why do talents come and go? I didn't know what to say. Then she laughed. A laugh that could be heard all the way back to the village but a laugh which filled the space between us with joy. It was infectious. I joined in. And then…we kissed.

Still holding me by the hand, she walked me out of the village. I'm not sure what we talked about. I'm not sure if we talked at all. I'm not sure that, if we did talk, I made any sense.

We came to a tiny chapel. Meg told me that it was where Kentigern's mother had landed. I had heard of him. He started a church in Glasgow. She also told me that the village was founded by St Serf and it was he who brought up Kentigern.

And beside the chapel was a grass embankment which almost had a notice saying 'Lie on me'. And then…we sat down.

CHAPTER EIGHT

My Meg

When our lips parted, her headscarf had fallen onto her shoulders revealing her fair hair. Her eyes danced, almost at the same speed as the shake of my hands around her waist. She laughed again, This time more controlled, more to herself.

"Well, I hadn't expected that from a Brother," she said through her smile.

"Lay Brother."

"All right." She leaned back onto the grass. With her left hand she patted the space beside her. "Lay, Brother". And she laughed again. We both did, but it didn't stop me joining her.

We kissed again.

Oh, I had been with girls before. Usually in the fields up at Brechin. But then it was more a rough kind of play. The play was rough and they were rough.

But she was beautiful. She allowed my hands to explore her body. Although small, her curves were womanly. In comparison to the roughness of her dress, her skin was so smooth. Every fibre of my being wanted to be at one with her. I leaned further across to fuse our bodies together. Suddenly she pushed me off and jumped to her feet and sorted her dress. Even in this quick movement, she was elegant compared to my awkward attempt to stand without displaying too much of my desire.

She laughed. She kissed me again and shook my hand – only it wasn't my hand.

"I like it when you stand up," she said with the laughter still punctuating her words. "Let's head back to the harbour." And with that she started walking.

It seemed as if nothing had happened. She was walking, pulling her headscarf up. My heart was beating too fast, my hands were still shaking and my body still showed signs of being in another emotional place.

“Don’t you want to come, Alan?” she shouted, still with that laughter in her voice. I caught up with her. I stopped her. I cupped her chin in my hand. I kissed her. This was my first kiss. The others we had just drifted into. This one I dictated. My left arm clamped her waist to me and my tongue explored her mouth. I was forceful, but it was how I felt.

When I released her, the laughter was gone. She stared at me, her blue eyes almost looking into my soul.

Eventually she said, “I should go now.” Her voice was softer, lower, less confident, more serious. I knew now was the time to say something important. I blurted out “Stay a bit.”

“I can’t.” Even softer, even lower. Then after a slight pause. “But I could come back over tomorrow.”

“Yes. Yes, yes, yes, yes.”

Her laugh returned with a vengeance. She grabbed my hand and started pulling me along as she started to run. There might have been ground, but my feet didn’t seem to touch it. All I could do was join her laughter and shout ‘Yes’ in increasing volume every five steps or so.

We ran. We reached the small harbour in no time. We didn’t talk – apart from my monosyllabic contribution of the affirmative. When she stopped, she looked up and this time she kissed me. Softly, gently as if her lips were trying to remember the indentations in mine. It was the other Meg again. No laughter. And those eyes, drilling into my very being, as if trying to pull my heart to hers.

“Go now. I have to finish my work here and catch the ferry.” And before I could say anything, she continued, taking charge, “Be here tomorrow at mid-morning.”

I simply nodded. I moved to kiss her again, but she put her finger gently to my lips to stop me.

“Tomorrow. Now, go.”

She waited until she saw her command had had some effect. I started my way up the hill. I turned several times to wave, but she didn’t. Then she disappeared behind the houses.

I know now the hill is fairly steep, but that day I didn’t. The footpath seemed to convey me itself until I arrived at the Abbey.

I hadn’t given John a thought. He might have left. I felt a twinge of guilt.

But I needn't have worried. The first person I saw on approaching the Abbey was John. He was sitting on the grass. I couldn't tell if he was contemplating. Doubtful. Or if he was asleep. More likely.

"John."

He slowly opened his right eye. "Alan. So whit ha'e ye been up tae?"

"Just down at the harbour."

"So whit's happening? Are ye findin' a ship?"

So that was what he was thinking I was doing. I hadn't even found out what the news of the day was or what ships had come in. "No, I told you. I'm travelling through England."

"And Ah telt ye that could be dangerous."

"I've got my letters of introduction."

"And just whit authority dae ye think the Abbot at Brechin has wi' his royal shit Edward? Dinna be daft, man. Find a ship frae here. The seas are more trustworthy than the English. Get back doon an' see who's heading fur Holland and make tae France frae there."

"I might, but I'm thinking of stopping here for a couple of days."

"So, whit has happened to ma Alan? Where is the impetuous youth that I ha'e come tae know? A sudden care fur yer horse?"

I hadn't thought of Meg. If I were to go by sea, I'd have to sell her and buy another when I got there. But I could ride south and keep Meg. I could delay my travels. I could spend more time with the other Meg. I could forget about France altogether!

"Too much thinkin', Alan" said John, giving reason to my delay in replying. "Share yer thoughts."

"No, it's nothing. I was just thinking about the journey."

There was a little silence between us. I don't know if he believed me. His eyes seemed to say "Aye, right" while what he actually said was:

"Ah'm off today. Need to get tae Dunfermline afore night. Come." He stood up slowly and again held my gaze. "Let's share some food an' drink before I leave."

"With salt?"

"With salt. Salt of the sea fur the salt o' the earth."

CHAPTER NINE

Meg Returns

We ate alone. The monks seemed either to be at prayer or working in the gardens. The food definitely tasted better with the salt, but the small ale didn't come up to John's expectations.

"Pish", seemed to cover it laconically.

He gathered up his stuff and collected his horse, neither of which took long. In the small entrance to the Abbey we stood looking at each other. Our time together had been short, and, while not uneventful, it had created a bond. We grabbed each other's right arms, being stronger than a handshake but not becoming an embrace. Neither of us spoke. I'm not sure if either of us knew what to say. Eventually:

"That sword, Alan. Keep it in its scabbard. Only take it out if ye really mean it."

Those eyes. For the second time that day I felt that someone could see inside me. I wasn't sure how literal to take his words.

"I'll look after it as I would a trusted friend."

"Aye, dae that, Alan. That business o' the other night. It's no' fur you tae worry aboot or even think on. A minor skirmish. But oor country's heading fur worse. We canna yet beat oor swords into ploughshares. Beware the common folk." Or did he say, Beware the Comyn folk?

He mounted his horse and with a "God be with ye. God speed" he was off.

Some moments in life seem important. And this one seemed important. I didn't really get to know John. For all he told me little, I knew there was something going on, some danger that lurked around him. For all we had spent only a little time together, he seemed to know what was going on in my mind. For all we had only been friends for a few days, it seemed the parting was too abrupt. I might never see him again. I might not live long enough to hear that rasping voice again. I might not be able to tell him about Meg. "Pish". I went back to the cell.

Day became night. And it was a long night. I'm afraid thoughts of John were not the reason. Nor the sleeping conditions more befitting a soldier from Sparta. It was Meg.

I relived the time we had spent during the day. I could still taste her lips. I could still feel her body. But would she come back? What if she wasn't there in the morning? How would I find her? I knew her name, but not that of her father. I knew where she came from, but not where she lived. If she didn't come, I would never find her again. She would be lost to me forever. At times it seemed sleep was the same.

Morning eventually came. It was one of the few times in my life when I appreciated being compelled to make early morning devotions. Sleeping ceased, prayers and hymns began. My prayers might have been directed to Our Good Lord, but their content was more temporal. My hymns might have evoked Our Dear Lady, but the Dear Lady had taken on a more temporal form. Meg, will you be there?

Breakfast was both a break of fast and fast. But I had still quite a time to spend before I met her. And times are so approximate. What was her mid-morning? Meg, will you be there?

I found myself back in the monks' garden watching them tending their crops. There was a quiet, serene air about their working. It seemed to contrast with the speed my heart was beating. While I was excited, they were calm. While I wanted the new sun to race across the sky, they wanted the sunlight hours to last long. I couldn't contain myself. I set off down the hill. I was sure I'd be early, but I was sure I wouldn't be late.

The harbour was much as I'd seen it the previous day. More boats were in. Some were being unloaded. Some had obviously come in with their fishing catch. Some, with sailors lounging around, were waiting on their goods to arrive. Everyone going about their normal day. None of them realising how important the day was.

I headed for the same rock where we had first met and sat down. It didn't feel just yesterday that I first met her. I started to relive the day with a smile. I started to think of this day with some trepidation.

A small rowing boat was just making its way into the harbour. And there, sitting on the back, was Meg –my Meg.

We both stood at the same time, waving. The only difference was that I was standing on terra firma. She nearly capsized the boat and was subject to a tirade from the ferryman. I ran down to the quayside and helped her off. The process developed into a hug and into an embrace and into a kiss. And then we separated, almost guiltily.

"So. my Alan. How are you today?" she asked.

Her shawl was over her shoulders and her hair seemed even more fair in the sunlight.

"Grand."

"Had a good morning?"

Was it just my imagination or had she tightened her clothes round her body? At any rate she seemed to have more curves than I could remember.

"Fine."

"What did you do?"

Could I put my arm back round her? Would she want that? Should I take her hand?

"Nothing, really."

She grabbed my hand – yes – and from her other hand thrust into mine a canvass bag, a weighty canvass bag.

"You carry the nails. Sounds like you need some iron."

And she was off. I followed, almost like a puppy, at her heels. Is it my imagination or am I seeing more of them today?

"Trade first, then lunch" she said, answering my unasked question. "I've got to deliver these and pick up my salt. Then we can have some lunch. They have good mussels here. But we have to do it fast. It's an early tide today and I can't miss the ferry back."

She led us west out of the village, keeping close to the river bank. She walked fast.

"When will he be leaving?" I ventured, referring to the ferryman who was less than pleased with her over exuberant waving of a few minutes ago.

"Mid-afternoon. Any later and the tide will push him too far upstream."

I was pondering how to say I was looking forward to spending more time with her, how I had postponed my journey, how... when she cut through my thoughts and thrust her hand into mine. Then she squeezed it.

"We'll just have to make best use of the time we have", she said without breaking stride. A couple of minutes later stopped abruptly. "Give me the nails. You sit down and wait here. I'll go in here and sell them. I'll be back soon."

And with that she headed into a sort of shack. By the wooden skeleton of the beginnings of a boat sitting outside, this was obviously the boat builder she had come to trade with. She had got ferried across the Forth from Faukirk with her wee bag of nails – well, quite a wee bag of nails – to sell them to this boat builder, to make enough money to buy some salt. Hard enough job today. About a league - maybe two hours rowing - but what about in the winter? A hard life. Maybe as hard as mine at Brechin.

I looked across the river, to the hills on the other side. My journey. In a way, when I crossed them I had left our high lands behind and, according to my maps, would be starting the journey to England. And then to France. But what about Meg? I can't just leave her now. But if I stay, what about my mission? If I stay, what would I do here? If I go, would I ever see Meg again? Is this 'new singing' more important than she? Is…?

She came back out of the ramshackled building her face lit up with her glorious smile. It was a smile which seemed to come from her inside, reaching her lips and then her eyes.

"Come, Alan. Let's get that salt and then something to eat."

We retraced our steps as she told me that she had got good siller for the nails. She saw that his supplies were almost out and had bargained for a better price than usual. The sun hadn't shifted much in the sky before we passed the harbour and reached some wet, open land by the river. This, she explained was where the monks made the salt. She left me again and, after some discussion with a monk, who I assumed was in charge, returned with two bags of the precious salt. Once again she was smiling that smile.

"Hold these. I'll be back soon."

Somehow I imagined everyone would just carry out her orders. I held the bags and waited. She returned carrying a reed basket.

"Freshly boiled mussels and todays' bread. Let's find a quiet place to eat." And then she kissed me.

CHAPTER TEN

Goodbye

She led me up through some woods until we came to a grassy clearing where the sun could just get through the trees. She sat down and laid the food on the grass. I sat beside her and laid my bags of salt on the grass. She started pulling the bread apart and, with one of the smaller pieces, began to feed me.

As I endeavoured to chew the bread, my tongue was soon licking the tips of her fingers. Now the process of eating didn't seem so important anymore. Without thinking, my arm encircled her waist and I was sure I felt a slight shudder tremble through her body.

From the tips of her fingers to her mouth. And this time it was a different kind of kiss. It wasn't brutal, but it was intense. It wasn't controlled, but it was passionate. I had never kissed or been kissed like that before. And yet, without thinking, without practise, our bodies had somehow become conjoined at the lips.

As we separated, my hand ran through her hair on the back of her head and we looked at each other without talking. She took my other hand and laid it just below her neck. As we kissed again, this time with our eyes open, it drifted to find the curves of her womanhood. No longer brutal, no longer passionate. But delicate, tender, as if my hand was trying to remember every contour. As my hand glanced across her tip, I felt that same slight shudder again. My own heart was beating fast. It seemed to be on a mission to send my blood quickly through my body and every extremity of my body reacted accordingly.

Our bodies were wrapped closely but I couldn't help still squeezing, trying to make the two bodies one. Meg took hold of my left hand and gently moved it from her waist to the top of her knee. As I explored the softness of her flesh, she put up no resistance. As my hand moved from the smoothness of her leg to the rougher texture of hair, there was more than a slight shudder.

Without thinking, I was lying on top of her. Without talking, she began helping me position things. Without flinching, she gave a little gasp on entry.

I remember the next few moments a little hazily. That it was magnificent, there was no doubt. There had been no better moment in my life than this. It seemed odd that, when it was over and we lay back, such a triumphal moment should be summed up with a "Thank you" from Meg. As I kissed her again, trying to let her feel the depth of my gratitude, the reply to her 'thank you' could have been 'from now on, I'll do anything for you'. But I said nothing.

My eyes closed as I lay back. The ground was soft. The sun was still shining. God was in his heaven.

"Mussels."

While I was tempted to take it as a compliment from Meg, I realised she had returned to our uneaten lunch. From Elysium to sustenance. We didn't talk too much. But at every chance, we squeezed hands or exchanged short kisses. From bliss to this.

"I have to go."

No. This has to last. This time must stretch.

"I'll miss the ferry."

"Why don't you just stay here?"

"And stay the night with you in the monastery? Alan, don't be so daft."

"We could find a place for you to lodge here."

"No, I have to go back. I have a father to look after."

"I see." I didn't. But I did realise how little we knew of each other. Time. I needed to find out more. I needed to share everything with this Meg. "Tomorrow? What time will you be across?"

"I won't be coming across?"

"Why not?"

"Because you have things to do."

In her pause, I thought 'what things?– Just tell me what they are and I'll do them. Then I'll see you'.

"You have to go to France."

"France!" France was the last thing on my mind. My journey wasn't important. Here. This was important.

"Yes, France. It is your duty. You must go. You cannot stay here. And if you do it will be without me."

"But I can't. I must stay here with you. Especially now. It's...it's important."

She kissed me again. "Yes, Alan, and you'll probably never know how important. Thank you."

How inadequate that phrase was. "Don't thank me, stay with me. Be with me."

"No, you must go to France and I must go to Faukirk. Some difference, eh? My father taught me duty and duty must come first. You go. But I'll wait. When you come back, you can find me. Maybe you could even take me to Brechin."

Although her lips parted at her attempt at levity, her eyes were no longer sparkling. While before they danced, now they had a depth.

I have never experienced such sadness. I knew from looking into those eyes that she meant what she said. I knew she would never change her mind. I knew I was losing Meg.

As we walked back to the jetty, we talked of how we would meet again. How I would find her. But we both knew that we were parties to a pretence. She kept telling me to look after myself on the journey. I told her how happy today had made me feel. She kept reminding me how important this new music was. I told her I would never forget her. She kept going over again that it was my duty. I told her we would meet again at the kirk in Faukirk.

As her boat pulled away from the shore, she didn't look back. I watched her wrapping her bags of salt in her shawl to protect them from the sea spray. I could only think that her mind had turned back to her business. I waited and watched as the ferry got smaller and the silhouette of Meg began to merge and become one with the ferry. I watched until I couldn't see my Meg but just shapes on the boat.

I turned to climb the hill back up to the Abbey. Such a short time in Cuilross. And yet, in that short time, I've said goodbye to two new friends. Both parting without much fuss. Both leaving my life. The difference was that one, in that same short time, had become a real part of my life, a part of me.

Each climbing step took me further away from the river, from the boat, from what should have been my life.

The wool on the right sleeve of my habit was going from damp to wet. My heart was wringing itself out.

CHAPTER ELEVEN

Call of Duty

It was a long night. There was little sleep. My thoughts were all of Meg. And of her father. It took a while before I realised I didn't know his name. How could I find Meg again if I didn't know her father's name?

The emptiness that I felt during the night became almost intolerable. It was not eased by the thought that on top of everything else I had sinned. Here I lay in a monastery as a sinner.

The sounds of the monks at prayer allowed me to shake off the night. I couldn't join them, but I washed and went to see the other Meg. I saddled up and took her for some exercise. It would provide an excuse for not appearing at breakfast.

Meg had obviously recovered. She was ready for the next journey. But what journey? I had letters of introduction to various people on my journey through England. One was to John Peckham, Archbishop of Canterbury. My abbot told me that he was an excellent maker of songs, even if he was Franciscan. But John had warned me of the troubles in England. He said I should ship from here to Holland. What then of Meg?

Aye, what then of Meg? Why is duty so important? Surely love should come before duty?

After stabling the other Meg , I walked again into the Abbey gardens. There too was Father Ambrose. He waved, stopped his work and came across to me. We sat on a bench and looked down at the river. Across that river was my life. Today it seemed so close. Yet Meg seemed so far away.

"And how is young Alan today?" What might have been regarded as a pleasantry of a question somehow felt more probing.

"Fine."

"Are you leaving us soon?"

"Probably."

“Duty calls?” It was as if he could see into my heart. No. it was as if he could see into my thoughts. Too many people seeing into Alan.

“Why does duty call, Father?”

“I know not the answer to that, Alan. It might be our conscience.”

“I do not understand.”

“I’m not sure I do too clearly,” he replied. “Let me try it this way. You see yon boat down there on the river?”

“Yes.”

“Well, its master has chosen its course. He has decided which way it should go. Sometimes the wind blows it off course, but he will rectify that. So, God has chosen our path and like that boat we must follow it.”

“It’s our duty to follow it?” Perhaps my words showed more understanding than my brain was comprehending.

“At the back of the boat there is a rudder. By altering it, the boat will change direction. Perhaps that rudder is our conscience. It should be able to keep us on the right heading.”

We sat for a moment or two in silence. Perhaps I was trying to understand what he was saying. Perhaps I was wondering how much I should tell him. I liked the wind that blew me off course and I wasn’t sure if I wanted the rudder to correct my path.

“I don’t want to go to France.”

Another silence.

“But your Abbot has sent you there. It is God’s will.”

“I was happy to go when he sent me. But things have changed. I…”

“Yes?”

“I have met someone.”

“And this someone doesn’t want you to go to France as you have been instructed?”

“She does, but….”

“There are no ‘buts’, my son. Pray to God. He will strengthen you. And do your duty.”

He rose as if he had said the final word on the subject.

“Father, I have sinned.”

“Then confess next year at Lent.”

"Would you here my confession now?"

"And would this sin be the reason for your change of heart? For the boat going off course?"

"Yes, Father."

He stood directly facing me and put his hands on my shoulders. His eyes once again pierced straight into my soul.

"Then we must help you", he said simply. "We cannot leave you in this state. Kneel down, my son."

"Shouldn't we go into the Abbey?"

"Here we are in God's great cathedral. Here we can conduct the sacrament of penance. The Abbey might be a little crowded for what you want to say and we don't need to make confession public."

I told him what had happened. Even the difficult bit. He listened but didn't show any emotion. He told me I required to have a year of solemn penance. That I should wear mournful garb, but that my habit would do. That I should be in poverty, but that I already was. I listened to him and didn't show any emotion.

"Go, my son. Go to France. Go do your duty." And he left me to resume his gardening. It was as if it wasn't very important to him.

But to leave Meg? As I walked back to the Abbey, I prayed a simple prayer. I know praying isn't like striking a bargain, but it was all I could think of at the time:

God, I'll go to France. I'll do my duty. I'll learn this new music. And then, you must help me find Meg again. Amen.

CHAPTER TWELVE

The Sea Calls

I walked back across to the Abbey. It was one thing deciding to go. It was another deciding how. My inadequate, incomplete prayer took me to the Chapel. I knelt and thought. The Abbot entered from the side door and, after kneeling before the Altar, came and sat beside me.

As I rose he said, "Yes, Alan, God will guide you."

"By giving me a better map?"

"No, by making His will clear. Follow me."

He led me to his cell and indicated that I should sit. These Cistercians knew how to treat themselves. No suspending myself against the wall as at Brechin, but an actual stool.

"So, when are you leaving us, my son?"

"Soon, I think. I don't know what to do next . I was going to travel through England. I have introductions to several Abbeys. But I've been warned that the journey might be too dangerous just now."

"You are right to be worried. Unsettled minds lead to unsettled times. So you might travel by sea?"

"It has been suggested, but I've never been to sea before."

"Why don't you go down to the harbour and see what ships are sailing? That might help you make up your mind."

I did as he suggested. The walk down hill seemed longer. My eyes kept looking across the river. Was there a ferry? Would Meg be on it? Was she looking across at me from the other side? But when I arrived at the harbour, there was no sign of a ferry and no sign of Meg.

I asked around to see what ships might be sailing to France. I was told to find Anald. The old fisherman telling me this had lost most of his teeth and I found it difficult to make out what he was saying. I thought he said I would find him in The Auld Hoose so I followed his pointing to a small house across from the pier. Asking for Anald got little response until a small, wizened man sitting in the corner of the tiny room twining a rope had the grace to say,

"Noo, would that be Ranald?"

"Yes, it might be. Do you captain the ship going to France?"

He put down the rope and ate some of the bread and cheese in front of him. As I sat beside him, he pushed the food towards me, though made no verbal offer to share.

"Who asks?"

"My name is Alan Murray. I'm trying to get to France."

"To what purpose?"

It could have been a long answer. Instead, I reckoned a simple question deserved a simple answer.

"To learn music."

For such a small man, his laugh was enormous. It echoed round the small room bringing out the brewster. If I sound knowledgeable now, I should explain that I learned this from Ranald. He told me that brewster was the name for the woman who brewed the ale and that I was in fact sitting in a Cauld Hoose, so called because she didn't serve any hot meals only cold food, not an Auld Hoose.

"He's travelling all the way to France to learn music," he told the others. I'm unsure why this caused general mirth, nor why the lady of the house found it particularly funny, but laugh they did,

"Have ye bin tae sea afore?" I could just about make out his question through his subsiding laugh.

"No."

"And ye're prepared to try it tae learn music?"

"Yes."

"Ye're either wrang in the heid or heid strong."

"Or I have to get to France."

"Alan was it?"

"Aye."

"Well, ah'm no gang tae France."

"No."

"Naw. Ah'm gang tae the Low Countries."

"Where abouts?"

"Ah was headin' tae Amsteldam, but ah'm hearn' they've a new dam at the River Rotte. I ha'e a ship laden wi' sheeps' wool. Ah'm telt we'll get good sillar oan it there."

"And can I get to France from there?"

"Man, it'll tak me a' ma time tae navigate the sea. Ah'm no' one that kens the land."

"If I can get to Paris from where you land, will you take me?"

"Aye, if ye have the sillar. Mind ye, this is a workin' boat. Nae nice stuff. Ye'll need tae bed wi' the crew?"

"And when do you sail?"

"The morraw. First tide."

After making arrangements to see him later in the day to confirm my trip – or otherwise - and after checking there was still no sign of Meg, I headed back to the Abbey. My plan was to discuss this new route with the Abbot and see if it was possible to sail the next day. If my plan was for discussion, the Abbott's was for resolution.

"So, a ship is sailing tomorrow. It's going to the Low Countries. You can be on it. God's will is done."

"But where is it landing? This place was not on my map."

"From the River Rotte you can make your way to Amiens in France. From Amiens about three days horse ride to Paris."

I guess he too had been at the Second Council in Lyons to have such knowledge of France. As if to underline God's will, he continued:

"I've found a buyer for your horse and I've sold your sword. I'll give you the gold for both and you can sew it into the hem of your habit. That way you'll have enough money for your journey when you land."

"My sword? I could still take that."

"My son, you'll be safer travelling just in your habit without bearing arms. France is probably safer than England, but safer still to travel as a man of the cloth, a man of peace."

He pulled out a small wooden box from under his table and found a key somewhere under his robe. He gathered some gold pieces and handed them to me.

"Here. That should cover your horse and your sword. Get the rest of what you need sorted out."

I took the gold but didn't tell him how heavy my habit would become. It already had some gold coins stitched in the hem on the orders of Friar William. Maybe they both had the same training. Maybe deviousness is a quality required of Abbots.

"Has Meg gone? My horse?" I asked.

"No, she's still in the stable."

"I'll go and see her."

"She'll be fine. She's going to a good home. Who knows, she might still be here when you come back."

Saying goodbye to a pig is one thing. Saying goodbye to my horse was another. Meg, the pig, Meg, the horse and Meg…Goodbye.

CHAPTER THIRTEEN

Reaching the Low Countries

It is perhaps best not to dwell too long on my sea crossing. The Good Lord gave man feet to walk the earth not to be at sea.

Ranald assured me this was a relatively new boat. It didn't look it to me. He took pride in explaining that his boat had a rudder at the back, a vast improvement on those with a rudder at the side. The boat was about fourteen paces long with a single central mast and sail. When you got below the deck, it seemed to be held together by cross beams, strategically placed to hit your head even in the necessary couching position.

Our beds were straw bags on the keel of the ship. They were placed at the side so that we could wedge ourselves in, but the clinker build of the ship meant that with, any movement, the planks dug into you and often left a deposit of wood sticking into your skin.

In the centre, still below the deck was the cargo. Hundreds of fleeces, held in place by ropes with ale kegs as weights. The fleeces were stinking, but their odour was often less disgusting than that emanating from the crew.

I could hardly imagine this boat staying afloat, let alone crossing the seas to the Low Countries. I had never been to sea before, and I never felt less inclined for my feet to leave Mother Earth. But set sail we did.

Within one day that talent I thought I had – strength – was flowing out of me into the ocean. If I went on deck, I suffered from the wind and sea spray. If I went below, I suffered from the stench and roll of the ship. I suffered. My prayers were not of me thanking God for me doing his will, but pleas for survival and an ending to the voyage.

Ranald was of little help. To every enquiry, he simply pointed right and said, "See yon coast? As lang as we can still see it, wir headin' weel. See yon sail, as lang as it's sittin' proud, we'll get there." I just offered more prayers and lost more strength.

Our arrival in the Low Country was not met with much acclamation. My arrival came with grateful prayers and great feeling for the land, which came to meet me rather than I to it.

In the time it took me to get my legs accustomed to solid earth, Ranald had been off selling his wool. Not only had he managed what by the smile on his face must have been a handsome price, he had sold his cargo to a merchant from Antwerp and had arranged with him to be my first mode of transport. How he managed this transaction is a mystery when even I, a fellow Scot, had difficulty in understanding his accent.

While my stomach revolted at having to spend more time with the stinking fleeces, my head told me it would be ungracious to reject the arrangement. And, as Ranald said,

"A've bin yon place afore. Frae there, ye'll get tae Paris. An' see oor Scottish silver pennies? They tak them here."

At least I wouldn't be needing my gold coins immediately.

I completed my farewells and carried out my introductions. The merchant's name was Henri from – well, I'm not really sure. After his fourth attempt at telling me, I just pretended to have understood.

It transpired that he had not bought the whole cargo. The crew had loaded his cart. It looked to me mountainously high even if the fleeces were secured by ropes. With the two of us sitting up front, Henri's poor horse was going to have a heavy load to pull. I wondered how Meg was. I wondered how both Megs were.

The long journey to Antwerp was uneventful. My non-conversational side had returned. On the boat, speaking was difficult if constantly interrupted with dashes to the side. On the cart with Henri, our gesturing skills weren't up to having much of a conversation. 'Paris' was understandable on both sides so at least he understood my intended destination.

When we arrived in Antwerp, he pulled up beside an enormous stone castle. He gestured for me to remain with the cart and disappeared up a small street. The castle was impressive and fairly newly built. Some-one around here had a lot of money.

Henri returned with a horse. As Ranald had said my Scottish silver pennies worked here. I understood his gesture of wanting payment so I got out my purse. This left my gold still intact. Henri helped himself to rather more than I would have wanted to give away then handed me the halter of the horse. He probably added a little to compensate himself for having an almost silent passenger.

I tried to gesture that I would like a saddle. Whether he understood or whether he knew not where to find one, the shrugs of his shoulders came to the same effect. Ah well, I used to ride bare-backed at home.

After much hugging and hand shaking, I mounted my horse. I tried to find out its name, but this only elicited repeated 'Henris'. Might as well just call him Henri then!

The real Henri just stood on the road, pointing and exclaiming,

"Paris, Paris."

A final wave and I was off – off to Paris. The fact that I had no idea how to get there didn't seem to worry my new friend Henri. As I rode away, I could still hear him shouting,

"Paris, Paris."

CHAPTER FOURTEEN

And on to Paris

My journey to Paris took me through the town of Ghent. I have never seen such a large town. But at least the long ride was helping me learn the language. I was even able to ask directions and managed to understand them without the pointing. I was also able to purchase a saddle. Riding in a habit is never easy. Riding in a habit bare-backed is akin to what they do to horses to stop them being the fathers of foals.

Then on to Lille. There I stayed at a Hospice run by nuns. A Countess Jeanne of Flanders had founded it in her own palace grounds. She even had the Coat of Arms of Flanders embroidered on the sheets. Sheets! I slept in a bed with sheets… and a blanket… and a pillow. With memories of Brechin and of the boat, this was even more special than their beautiful food.

Then through Amiens. I say through, but I really stayed a little longer than was absolutely necessary to rest Henri. And who wouldn't? Their new cathedral was stunning. It is difficult to describe. So large. So high. So beautiful.

I thought our tower at Brechin was impressive. It was very tall and had seven landings, but this was something else.

I walked down the nave. I paced it out. It took 135 paces from one end to the other. I couldn't work out the height, but it soared to the heavens. The vaulted ceiling was painted red and ochre. The floor had a labyrinth pattern that worshippers followed on their knees. In a true sense, I felt nearer to God in this place.

But what really held me back was meeting one Guillaume from the town of Amiens. What a fascinating man. He is a painter, but, more than that, he is a singer. I spent time listening to his songs. He writes them himself and the words, so I suppose he's a poet as well. The French call him a trouvere. To be truthful, he hasn't a great voice, but his tunes were new and exciting. And they weren't religious!

He also had a way of writing the music down so that he could remember his tunes. I could see how his marks went up and down depending on whether he was singing high or low. It was very clever. Although I could follow his marks, they weren't enough for me to sing them by myself. But Guillaume could follow them and knew exactly how long each note was. We must learn from this. All our music has to be learned by listening to someone and copying them. This could be much better.

On my last night he took me to an inn. We had lots of wine. He sang his songs. They got louder as the night progressed. I sang mine. But his songs seemed much more fitting to the occasion than my hymns. But he copied what I was singing. He learned so fast. Then he made his marks to remind him of my tune later. Yes, this could be much better.

And then Paris.

If I thought Ghent was big, Paris was even bigger. It took me a little time to get to know it. On the right bank of the river was where all the merchants were. On the left bank were the students and academics. The city itself was really on an island in the middle of the river – the Ile de la Cite -accessed by a bridge.

It was to the city that I first headed as I could see the towers of Notre Dame. And what a sight it was. Those two towers heading to the heavens, but somehow still solidly rooted to the earth. The carvings round the doors. And these long windows.

Although I stayed in Paris for about three months and although I was in this church every day, there was always something new to discover. They had been building this place for a hundred and fifty years, and indeed were still building, but it was as if every day of that time brought another piece of beauty to the glory of God.

Outside the church, it was much the same. Building work everywhere. They were building ramparts round the city. And something really new. The King had ordered paving to be laid on the streets. I had never seen that anywhere before.

But it wasn't only the building work that impressed me. People from every country seemed to be here. Students from many nations. Academics arguing with each other in different languages. On the other side of the river it seemed that there was nothing you couldn't buy. This was not just a new country, this was a new world. Oh, if only Meg was here to see it all. To see the structures her nails could support. And for me to see her beauty against the beauty that was all around me.

And then there was the singing.

CHAPTER FIFTEEN

A Paris Hostelry

Ah yes, there was the singing.

The choir at Notre Dame rehearsed every day. If there was beauty in the buildings around me, the beauty in this music surpassed it. It was so new, but it was so beautiful. The way it echoed round the high roof of the cathedral. The way different voices carried different tunes. The way the notes blended to make a perfect sound.

Of course I learned about Leonin who was at Notre Dame a hundred years ago and who was the first to use different tunes at the same time. But it was Perotin who was responsible for this music. His music had three or four lines of singing at the same time. I had never heard anything like it. Four voices singing together. I was lucky as my voice is fairly high, so I always got one of the top lines. They called it the discant.

There was so much to learn. Not just the tunes but the special words they used to describe the different types of music. The motetus, the triplum, the quadruplum. And the one I really liked – the hoquetus. In French it means hiccup. In singing, it meant the music bouncing between the various parts.

Then there were the different rhythms. Sometimes a long note followed by a short one. They used three different lengths of note – a long, a breve and a semibreve. They tried to make the length of the music notes fit the words. They had other names like ‘perfect’ and ‘tempora’ and ‘tempus’. When you were singing, you soon got to know what they meant.

But the most surprising thing of all was to sing in French. They had songs where some of the words were sung in Latin with French being used by some singers at the same time. This was not just beautiful, it was exciting.

And then the most exciting of all. We sang everywhere but not just in Notre Dame. When we were in a hostelry, we would sing songs which weren’t religious. And they would be all in French.

I'm not sure what Friar William would have made of it back in Brechin. I'm not sure if that was really why I was here. But I am sure it was the most fun anyone could have singing.

One night a few of us were over in a hostelry on the left bank. It was filled with students of many different nationalities. It was not a quiet place.

I had been told before about a previous Bishop of Frascati. A name like Jacques de Vitry. He had seemingly written what he heard the students of Paris saying when he had been there. They called the English drunkards, the sons of France effeminate, the Germans obscene. The Burgundians stupid, the Bretons fickle, the Lombards vicious, the Romans seditious, the Sicilians cruel and the Flemish slothful. I remembered thinking at the time, 'I'm glad they didn't reach the Scots!'

Well, the company on this night seemed to contain a bit of all these. I'm not sure how many were from Lombardy, but there was a feeling that any moment a fight would break out.

We started to sing a kind of love song. It might alter the mood a little. At the start, everyone quietened down and listened. However, whether our songs were not obscene enough for the Germans or were too much about woman for the French, it wasn't long before their noise indicated that our singing wasn't appreciated. With that, our company broke up. Our ale was usually paid for from the coins given to us from those appreciating our entertainment. There would be few ales tonight.

Having bid farewell to my fellow choristers, I decided on one more ale before heading to my lodgings. Our host poured it with some dexterity and engaged me in conversation while topping up my flagon.

"And where are you from, young man?"

"Scotland."

"Scotland is it. We had one of you fellow countrymen here last night."

Of course I had met other Scots in Paris. Not many, though. But there is something about meeting someone from your country when you are abroad that makes it special.

"And his name?" I asked.

"Never asked. Just as I've never asked yours. Safer. He's been in here for a few nights now."

He passed over my ale and I moved to find a seat. The only one available was near the back of the hostelry, but at least away from the most raucous group of students. The candle on the barrel that served as my table was almost out. The end of another Meg?

What was Meg doing now? Still selling her nails? Still picking up her salt? For all the excitement of this Paris, I missed her terribly. She should be here with me. She should hear me singing with the others. I should be holding her. I should be sleeping with her.

My eye caught a new customer heading to get served. He was tall.

"Here's your man, " shouted the landlord.

After a few minutes of unheard conversation between this new customer and the landlord, he picked up his flagon and headed towards my table.

As he walked, I noticed he had a slight limp and his right shoulder drooped a little. The man from Dundee.

Since living in Paris, I had stopped wearing my habit in favour of street clothes, though we always wore our robes when singing in Notre Dame. Perhaps he wouldn't recognise me. I was dressed differently and it was quite dark where I was sitting. He pulled up a stool.

"Aye," he said.

"Aye," I replied, thinking back to when conversation didn't come easily to me.

"Where ye from?"

"Brechin. You?"

"Around. Born in Stirling."

Both of us savoured our ale, as if the next swallow would create the next question.

"Have ah met you before? Ah usually ken a face."

An answer in the affirmative didn't seem the best idea. An answer in in the negative might come back to haunt me, as well as being a lie. I went for something more obscure.

"I've been in Paris several months, but I'm sure I've never bumped into you here. Have you been here long?"

"Naw, jist a few days."

We both drank again. This time, however, I'm sure we both hoped the next swallow would avoid the next question.

"And yer business here?" he asked eventually.

"Singing."

You could almost see his right shoulder droop even more as he relaxed after my answer. Singers, apparently, aren't a threat.

"At Notre Dame?"

"Aye, at Notre Dame."

"So yer a priest then?" Of course, I was dressed in my street clothes. Last time he saw me I was in my habit. He might recognise a face but obviously the garb dulled his senses.

"No – just learning to sing."

"Well, my singer from Brechin, this requires another ale. Let it not be said that those of us frae Stirling are tight wi' oor sillar."

And so he left to have our tumblers refilled. I was smiling to myself at having navigated the conversation so well. He returned with our full glasses and shoved mine across the table, We drank again in silence.

To make conversation I asked, "And what's your business in Paris?"

My navigation skills had just failed.

CHAPTER SIXTEEN

Meeting Again

It was as if a cold wind had entered the place. The chill seemed to reach freezing. Not a muscle in his body moved and his eyes gave me a fixed stare.

It wasn't the look Meg gave me, or Father Ambrose, when I felt they were looking into my soul. It was the kind of look I would have got if had sworn in Notre Dame.

Another silence.

"Ma business is ma business be it in Stirling or in Paris."

"Of course," I said. "To be honest, I was just making conversation."

Another silence. But this time it was different. It was as if he was weighing me up. Could I be trusted?

"How much news do ye get from Scotland?"

"Not very much. Just some from the odd traveller like yourself."

"Ye'll hae heard their ca'ing John Balliol spineless."

I had. While I was here in Paris, John Balliol was crowned King of Scotland. Before his crowning, Edward of England, acting as the Lord Paramount of Scotland, made him swear an oath of allegiance. But only a month after becoming King, Edward made him swear another oath of allegiance. The King of Scots promising allegiance to an English monarch! We might as well just be part of Edward's Kingdom rather than our own nation.

"Yes, I've heard some people are calling him that."

"Aye, weel they might hae tae find another name soon."

"Because?"

He took another swig from his tankard.

"Yer name?"

"Alan, Alan Murray."

"Weel, young Murray……"

"And yours?" I interrupted.

"Campbell, Fraser Campbell."

"I'm pleased to meet you, Mr Campbell."

"Some say it's derived from the Gaelic."

"I'm sorry. What is?"

"Ma name – Campbell. Some say it means 'crooked mouth'. But there's nothing crooked coming oot o' ma mouth now."

He paused again. He placed his tankard back on the table with more force than perhaps was necessary. He leaned forward.

"Are ye a talkative lot in Brechin?"

"I wouldn't say so," I replied, hardly understanding him.

"Ye'd better no be. For what Ah'm aboot tae tell ye goes no further than yersel'."

Then he began to tell me things that would change the rest of my life.

Edward had given our King until the first of September to raise Scottish troops for his invasion of France. He needed help as he was still occupied dealing with the Welsh. Balliol had returned to Scotland and, with other nobles, the decision was made to defy Edward. 1294 would be a very important year for the Scots.

But before the deadline, Balliol had to secure friends. Some nobles were trying to get King Eirik II of Norway to lend money and some battleships. Others were despatched to France to plead with King Philip. Fraser Campbell.

"And did you meet with King Philip?" I asked after his story seemed to have reached a natural end.

"Naw. But with some of his court. Ah think we might get a Treaty oot o' it."

"For the French to help us?

"Aye, but for us to invade England if the English take on the French. It would give Edward two fronts tae worry aboot."

"And when will the Treaty be signed?"

"There's still mair negotiation. Philip wants his neice tae marry Balliol's son Edward. Ah'm returning wi' some likenesses o' her."

I'm not sure what force made my decision. I suddenly just felt compelled to return to Scotland. Of course I'd had letters from Abbot William asking about my progress and wondering when I might be returning. Of course I had learned enough of the singing here to teach the others back home. Of course I wanted to get back to see if I could find Meg. I hadn't been with a woman during my whole stay in France. But none of these things had made me decide to leave. And yet, here, after a conversation with a stranger, albeit a Scottish one, I knew I had to leave – now.

"Can we travel back together?" I asked.

I may not have come to like my new companion, but the dangerous man of Dundee had receded. And in any case, the road would be safer with Fraser Campbell beside me. Apart from being an emissary from the Scots nobles, he was a daunting figure to look at. Aye, safety, and you never know I might get to actually like him.

But there was yet another pause.

"We can. But only as far as Stirling, efter that yer on yer own." And he burst out laughing. He filled the tavern with his raucous laughter. It was so infectious I had to join in, even though I thought his joke was a weak one.

"Mair ale, my young travelling companion?"

"Mair ale," I replied.

I was going home – to Brechin, to Scotland and, perhaps, to Meg.

CHAPTER SEVENTEEN

Bad Tidings

But going home was not easy.

Of course I had to organise the things I had to take back. Not only the notes – in both senses of the word – of what I had learned (thank you, Guillaume), but also deciding what to take for the journey. But my organisation was done much faster than Campbell's. Everything seemed to be taking so long to reach agreements. Diplomacy is not a fast art. Messages had to be sent from Paris to Scotland and back, so every stage took weeks. Then seemingly Philip took his time considering things before raising another question. And so it went on.

But things were moving a mite faster on our island across the sea.

King Edward had discovered what Ballol had been up to and that the Treaty between France and Scotland had been agreed. He was not best pleased. Seemingly he had begun to move some troops to his northern border in case we Scots started an invasion. Not content with that, he started building up his troops on his side of our border. Travel overland was out of the question. Travel by sea would be distinctly dangerous.

During all this time, Fraser was keeping me abreast of all developments at Court. More importantly, he was receiving intelligence as to what was happening in England. The omens were not good.

Eventually Fraser decided that he had to return and that it was time for our departure. It was still not safe, but the journey had to be made.

I was grateful that he made all the decisions for us. My job was just to agree with him. He decided when we should leave. He decided where we should leave from. He decided tomorrow was the day – 15th December, 1295. And we would leave from Amsteldam.

As it turned out, his choice of departure port was good. The small fishing village had been granted rights not to pay taxes. As a result, it's trade was increasing and plenty of ships were heading there with their goods, including those from Scotland. His timing, however, was less good. As we travelled to the port, we learned that Edward had seized all of King John Balliol's lands in England. Worse, when we arrived at Amsteldam, Fraser found out that King Edward had ordered more than two hundred of his subjects in Newcastle to form a militia. He had set a deadline of March. Everything felt that war was approaching. This made Fraser all the keener to set sail. This made me all the more anxious. Not just anxious about possible forthcoming events, but anxious about setting sail in the middle of winter. The sail to get to the continent had been bad enough, but to tackle the Northern Sea in the middle of winter with the possibility of the most violent storms seemed foolhardy at the least and more likely suicidal.

Fraser was getting more and more impatient. No ships were arriving or leaving for Scotland. Sure, we could have got one to England but even Fraser thought that impractical. It was now February and we still were in the Low Countries.

There is nothing to do in what was really a small fishing village in the middle of winter. Most days I went over my notes to ensure I would remember all of the tunes. My notation was fairly accurate, but sometimes I had to fill in from memory. On these occasions I made further notes. The harmonies were difficult when I only had my own voice. I tried to get Fraser interested but his lack of interest combined with his lack of singing prowess made it a pointless exercise which neither of us fancied repeating. .Eventually I trained myself to hold one note in my head while singing others. This way I was able to expand the notes I had. But still the time hung very heavily.

Fraser was like a stag in rut. His impatience showed in his temper and he was ready to lock horns with anybody. Even his limp seemed to get worse. I wasn't sure what was worse – him waiting for emissaries bearing news or him getting news that he didn't want to hear.

Eventually it seemed we were ready to set off. The waiting was over. Scotland beckoned. Then even worse news.

Edward had started assembling a fleet of ships off Newcastle.

This was devastating to Fraser. Here was Edward assembling an army and a sea army for an invasion of Scotland. But not just that. Any voyage we took from Amsteldam, not setting down on the English coastline, would mean having to pass Edward's fleet at Newcastle. It was unlikely that any Scots captain would take the risk of being stopped and boarded by Edward's troops. More delays. And delays when we both wanted to be back home.

From the moment I had asked him if we could travel back together, my thoughts seemed to focus back to Scotland. I had completed my business in Paris. I had learned all I could. And I wasn't so sure how important music was now. My country was being ruled by a King in name only. Edward had the upper hand. We were dancing to his song and that didn't make good music. I wanted to be back home.

I had never forgotten Meg. And I had never shared those special moments I had with her with any other woman. But since I had asked Fraser if we could travel back together, my thoughts seemed dominated with seeing Meg again. I wasn't sure how I could manage it, but I was sure it could only be managed when I was in Scotland. I wanted to be back home.

With each passing week, the news got worse. With each passing week, our impatience grew. By the end of March, the Earl of Buchan, John Comyn, had led the Scots to Carlisle. He couldn't breach the town walls, so he headed for the surrounding countryside burning and looting all that came before him before retreating to Scotland. Edward led his army, the letters said it had thirty thousand foot soldiers and five thousand cavalry, to Berwick. The citizens there turned down his offer of unconditional surrender. Edward overran the town. In three days, some twenty thousand of its citizens, including babies, children and women, were slaughtered by the English troops. Such revenge, such carnage. And we were stuck here in Amsteldam.

Fraser had changed from a rutting stag to a stag who knew his time was coming to an end. Depression hung over him like a cloud. And that cloud rained more and more ale down his throat. He would have done anything to get back to our homeland.

There was some good news when we heard that our King sent an envoy to Edward to tell him he was renouncing his allegiance. The envoy was the Abbot of Arbroath who was only 12 miles down the road from my Abbot at Brechin. John Comyn also led a force into the north of England which, by the accounts we had, left a trail of destruction behind them.

We heard that Edward had sent the Earl of Surrey, John de Warenne, to deal with the Scots. He seemingly met the Scots near Dunbar, at the foothills of the Lammermoor Hills. Comyn was again leading the Scots troops but, mistaking an English manoeuvre for a retreat, he ordered a charge. He was outflanked and some one hundred and thirty Scots knights were captured.

Our castles were falling to the English – Dunbar, Roxburgh, Jedburgh, Dumbarton, Edinburgh and Stirling. The English marched on through Scotland.

Whether it was the accumulation of bad news, or the fact of Scotland being invaded, I don't know, but Fraser stopped drinking. And with his abstinence came a decrease in his melancholy. To be replaced by that stag, by that bull of a man who was set to free Scotland single-handed. The heavens echoed to his bellowing and with each roar my spirits soared. The old Fraser was back.

I know not where he got the money nor where his gift of persuasion came from, but he bought a boat and a crew. Yes, he bought a boat. If no-one would carry us to Scotland, he would become an owner and sail himself. The deal he made with the captain was that, if he got us to Scotland, the boat was his. For this the captain furnished a crew, provisioned the boat, checked his charts and the weather and told us we could sail. After all this time in the Low Countries, we were going home.

I was going home – to Brechin, to Scotland and, perhaps, to Meg.

CHAPTER EIGHTEEN

Back Home

We sailed at the end of June, in the year of Our Lord 1296.

Although I wished to return home with every part of my being, my memories of the voyage that got me here were all too fresh, albeit a large time had passed. But my concerns did not become reality. The boat Fraser now owned was larger. When last time I had to wedge myself between the timbers to sleep, this time Fraser and I shared a sleeping area. When last time the boat was loaded with smelling fleeces, this time the captain had used barrels of water as ballast. It was not his intention to pull into an English harbour to replenish water. Fraser and I agreed.

The weather was fair and the sail was almost enjoyable. After these long months stuck in Amsteldam, there was a feeling of purpose, of doing something.

As we sat on deck each day, Fraser and I talked. Well, mostly Fraser talked, and I listened. He talked of our country, of our recent history. Of course, I'd heard a lot of it before as we passed the weary hours waiting before our journey. But when he talked before, often in drink, it was always with sadness and regret. Now he talked with energy. That feeling of purpose had enveloped him. He said it was time for change, Although he had been sent to Paris to represent Balliol, he no longer thought that Ballol could lead Scotland. We needed to find a new leader. One who would lead our army. One who would unite the barons. One who would send the English back south. His talk was infectious and I found myself agreeing with him more and more.

There was some debate as to where we should make landfall. Initially the Captain suggested Berwick as one of the first ports he would reach in Scotland. The earlier he could disembark us, the sooner the boat was his. But as Fraser pointed out, Berwick could still be in the hands of the English and our welcome was not guaranteed. More ports were discussed – St John's Town, Dundee - , but eventually it was decided we should land at Erlesferie. The Captain had landed there before as it was where he had sailed to set down pilgrims for the start of their pilgrimage to St. Andrews. Fraser liked the idea. Erlesferie was at the mouth of the River Forth, but on the opposite bank from Berwick. From there we could easily get to Dunfermline or cross the Forth further up to get to Edinburgh. But, almost more importantly, Erlesferie was a tiny village. No soldiers would be there, neither Scots nor English. We would be able to find out what was going on before heading to a safe destination.

Getting off the boat wasn't quite as bad as my arrival in the Low Countries. I regained my land legs quickly and it wasn't long before we were waving farewell to an erstwhile Captain but now a proud boat owner. It was a good feeling. My feet were walking on Scottish earth again.

The village was tiny. So small that it was difficult to find lodgings. We ended up on a farmstead just outside of the village. We soon established that there was little knowledge in the village of what was happening elsewhere. This information was essential to us before we could decide on the next stage of our travels. Fraser would need to send letters to find out what was going on and where. Send letters!

The farmstead had no vellum nor ink. So, as he went to the next market, the farmer had instructions to purchase some. But once again this would take time. We had the feeling we had exchanged Amsteldam for Erlesferie. One small village for another with nothing to do but wait.

At least I was able to help with some preparation. I fashioned some pens. It was one of my jobs at the Abbey in Brechin to make the pens for the monks. You start with a goose feather. You strip the feathers off, then you put it into hot sand. This makes it stronger and less brittle. Then you carve the end to a point and put a slit up the point. So Fraser had pens but we still had to wait for the rest.

I wanted to head off to Brechin, but Fraser said I should wait until we knew where the English armies were and who was in charge of what castles. My thoughts were Brechin first, then Faukirk. I had someone to find and now she was closer. But we waited. This was a condition we had both got used to.

Eventually the letters were written and the wait began for the replies. When the replies came, the news couldn't have been worse.

We were told that King John Balliol had written to Edward asking forgiveness for what he had done and saying that he would relinquish his crown. Another letter told us that he had abdicated in front of the Bishop of Durham, one Antony Bek. Our King seemingly wore a simple white robe and carried a white rod, like a penitent. And where did this happen? Brechin – my Brechin. Fraser had been right to delay my journey. The King of Scots surrendering to the King of England.

The final letter bore even worse news. Edward had had the Stone of Destiny moved from Scone to England – our informant knew not where. The Stone of Destiny was where our Kings were crowned. Some said it had been Jacob's pillow when he saw the angels of Bethel. Others say that it was brought from Antrim and placed on Moot Hill by the King of Dalriada. Whatever the truth, it was the symbol of our Kingship and Edward knew that. The crowning stone of the King of Scots stolen by the King of England.

If Fraser was a stag in Amsteldam, he became a lion in Erlesferie. I said as much to him. His reply was a little odd.

"Son, it's they English that are lions. They got wan fur Henry an' wan fur the next Henry's woman and wan fur Richard – the wan they cried Lionheart. It'll tak a big lion tae chase them three back home."

"I'm not sure I understand."

"Nae matter. Ah've been thinkin'. We canna sit here ony longer. We've got tae find ithers who are thinking o' joinin' the chase. Ah'll stand a better chance o' findin' what's what in Stirling. We'll head fur there. We'll go tae Dunfermline first and then make oor way tae Stirling."

"I should be heading for Brechin."

"Alan, there'll be a time fur music, but it's no noo. Ye can sing when Scotland's free. But first we hae tae mak it free."

I hesitated before replying.

"Weel?"

"Aye," I said. "Let's make Scotland free."

CHAPTER NINETEEN

Meeting an Old Acquaintance

Decision made, there was nothing that could stop Fraser leaving as soon as possible. In a day he had organised horses and sorted out what we should need. It was only a shortish journey to Dunfermline, but he seemed to be organising for a longer journey.

We took our leave of our host and started off. I raised the question of where we might stay. Fraser thought that finding lodgings in such a big town wouldn't be a problem. I suggested we might try the Abbey. I had heard of it before. I thought it was Benedictine. Something about it being a Priory for nuns before it became a monastery.

"D'ye think ah'd stay in a religious place? It might feel all right for you, but Ah'd be happier closer to iniquity." He laughed that laugh I'd heard before. It was like the old Fraser was returning. The Fraser with less of a limp, less of a stooped shoulder and more of a laugh. Purpose was returning.

"I understand that," I said, "but there are other considerations apart from your sins of the flesh. An Abbey would give us sanctuary. I mean, just in case we need it."

His laughing stopped and we rode along for a little while in silence.

"Ye know, Alan, yer right. Let's see if ye can get us into the Abbey."

Even the sure decision-making of Fraser had returned.

As we reached the Abbey, the sun was beginning to set. It looked imposing, though it's towers were only about the size of a man sitting on another man's shoulders. Not quite as imposing as my tower at Brechin. We headed into the courtyard and dismounted, looking around for someone to talk to but the place was quiet. Then one monk appeared from the direction of the cloister. Fraser shouted, "Ho" to attract his attention. He turned and pulled his hood form off his head. Even in the gloaming, there was no doubt who this monk was – John. John Blair.

Fraser must have recognised him too. They both stood still, facing each other. Neither moving, neither speaking.

"Weel, Alan, the years havnae improved yer taste in company," John said, breaking the silence.

I moved towards him with apprehension. I needn't have worried. We embraced each other like father and son. "This is Fraser," I said.

"Aye", he replied.

They faced each other again. "Campbell, Fraser Campbell", he said, but neither stretched out a hand in greeting.

"Are ye a King's man?" asked John.

"Would that we had a King", was his reply, "but no' that one."

"Aye, no' that one."

I called Fraser a stag before. Well, here we had two stags. It was as if they were deciding whether there was a prize worth fighting for. Without a hind in sight, it was Fraser who broke first.

"We need a new King, a new leader. We need wan that'll put yon Edward in his place – England."

I hadn't realised I had been holding my breath. I felt a deep exhale when John said:

"Ye canna be put up in the Palace, but I'll sort ye out in the Dormitory. Then it's tae the Refectory fur some food. Ye'll be needin' that efter yer journey."

It didn't take long to organise our bedding. John was right. We wanted to get some food. We joined the other monks at the long table. It was a Wednesday so no meat. They gave us a pottage. It was very grey looking, so I guess it was made from grey peas. It seemed to be thickened with bread and had small green bits in it, cabbage I guessed. While hardly the best meal we had had, it was at least better fare than on the boat and, as we were hungry, we emptied the bowls if not with relish, with speed.

It was Fraser who opened the conversation.

"So, who are ye fur – fur King?"

"Wheesht, man" said John. "Later."

Later came when we were in the Cloister and no other monks were around. John started with, "Ye ken Edward has left us wi' wan o' his people in charge?"

"Aye", said Fraser. And yes we had heard while we were stuck in Amsteldam.

"He goes by the name John de Warenne. Ah'm told that Edward appointed him warden of the kingdom and land of Scotland. Rumour hath it that Edward told him, 'he who rids himself of shit does a good job'. He did a good job for Edward against the Welsh so noo us turds have him to keep us in oor place."

"But it's oor place and oor land. What right has Edward tae think we're pairt o' his kingdom?"

"What right indeed?" echoed John.

You could almost feel a bond was forming between the two men. Two men who two hours ago might have been locked at each other's throats were quickly finding out how much they agreed with each other.

"I'm leavin' tomorrow to meet up with an old friend", said John. "A friend who has a band of fellows with him. He's already had some skirmishes with the English and he intends to have more. He might be the man."

"A friend to be trusted?" asked Fraser.

"Ah'm sure o' that. Mind you, when I say friend, I haven't seen him since we were at school thegither. But ah here tell he's fearless. Aye, an' just."

"Is he raisin' an army?"

"Ah'm no sure. He's certainly raisin' havoc. Ah'm no necessarily joinin' him. Ah'm more seein' the lie of the land. Want tae join me?"

Fraser looked at me. I hadn't known John Blair for long on our first meeting and only for a few hours this time, but I was sure he was someone who could be trusted. He was a monk after all. Our previous journey together had been safe. No reason to think this one would be otherwise. And if John felt this man was someone who could dent Edward's hold over Scotland, then why not meet him. I nodded to Fraser.

Fraser seemed to grow to his full height. "Weel, we could travel wi' ye. How far's the journey?"

"Ah'm told that he's at Gargowans, a little west of Stirling."

"No' that far."

I had no idea of the geography of the area but as Fraser was from Stirling I guessed his 'No' that far' would be accurate. Fraser looked again at me, perhaps aware that my nod had been my only contribution to the conversation.

"Ah said ah'd get ye tae Stirling. Ye comin wi' us?"

Since setting off for Dunfermline, and although my knowledge of the area was poor, I did know I was heading in the direction of Faukirk. Meg had been in my mind all day. I could find her then, when the time was right, we could go back to Brechin.

"Of course I'm coming."

Fraser's laugh erupted again. He scooped both of us into his body with his outstretched arms. No longer a father/ son greeting, this was men sharing a moment.

"Some ale is required," laughed John, leading us back into the precincts of the Abbey.

"Of course it is," agreed Fraser, accepting there were still some pleasures of the flesh to be had in an Abbey. "And his name, this school friend of yours?"

"Wallace. William Wallace."

CHAPTER TWENTY

Meeting a New Acquaintance

Having broken our fast, it seemed that John had been up earlier and had found new mounts for us. There was some personal pleasure, which I didn't share with others, in finding out that my horse was called Henry. Antwerp seemed so long ago.

The ride to Gargowans was some 30 miles, but our journey took longer as, without knowing who was in charge of Stirling Castle, John thought it advisable to take a longer route round. As we travelled, John and Fraser rode side by side. Though riding behind them, I could sense that the unease of their meeting yesterday had disappeared and had been replaced by the beginnings of camaraderie.

On a stop to partake of some victuals, I tentatively raised a question that had been bothering me.

"How do we find Wallace?"

"I think we will not find him," replied John. "I think he will find us. We will make a temporary camp and set a fire. That should be enough to alert him. My guess is he will send some of his men out to investigate in case we are some English scouting party. Yon man's no' daft."

It was almost exactly as John has foretold. We stopped outside the village and made a fire to cook our evening repast. In no time at all, there was a shout from that trees behind us.

"Ho, strangers, may we join you?"

Fraser replied with, "All good men are welcome."

Three of them rode in. Two dismounted leaving the third to tend their horses.

"Fair weather", one of them said.

"Aye, it is that," said John, his eyes darting between each of them.

"Little need for a fire then." It wasn't so much a question as a statement, but John replied anyway.

"Yer right, nae need fur warmth. But we intend tae cook."

"Your voices say that you're from around these parts." Another question phrased as a statement. This time it was Fraser who replied.

"Aye, ah'm a Stirling man. And yersels?"

"So what brings you to Gargowans?"

And that was a question – a very direct question. John's reply was not so direct.

"We travel for friendship."

The questioner looked at his companion, almost bidding him to enter the verbal fray. He took up the challenge.

"And is this arrow of friendship aimed in any particular direction?"

Some of the songs I had learned in France were about friendship, but arrows were never involved. Sometimes in love songs, but…

"It's flight will take us tae our target," said John.

This verbal thrust and parrying didn't seem to be advancing our cause, but it did seem to be making our guests more uncomfortable. Perhaps John, sensing they were running out of questions, or statements or illusions, thought it was time for a more direct approach.

"Ye kin see we carry no weapons. We canna be a threat tae anyone. I was told an old friend o' mine might be in these pairts."

"Aye, an' who might that friend be?"

From John's direct approach came the direct question. They have judged our voices as not being English. They have ascertained we are not armed. They can see by our dress that we are not soldiers. It seemed John now felt secure enough to answer.

"Wallace."

A quick look between them and a nod which was almost unseen.

"Then why not follow us?"

Fraser quickly stamped out the fire while I untied our horses. We were mounted almost as quickly as them and we set off riding three abreast with our new companions leading. It wasn't long before we had to adjust to single file as we rode through a fairly dense forest. It also wasn't long before we could hear the sound of men's voices in the evening air. And then, as we came out of the forest, there they were. I would say some sixty men.

The one leading us dismounted and indicated we should do likewise. He pointed the way forward. All of us noted that this time his pointing was done with his unsheathed sword. While we had not been assessed as a threat a short time ago, it seemed that chances could not be taken now.

A tall man rose from the centre of the group of men. Tall? He was a giant. He was not armed. But then, as all those surrounding him seemed to have a surfeit of arms, perhaps it wasn't necessary. And, in any case, apart from being tall, his own arms seemed like thick tree branches.

"Gentles, what brings you this way?"

John stepped forward. If he had hoped for immediate recognition, it wasn't to be. Perhaps his beard changed the image of the once schoolboy. He then announced his presence.

"William. It's John Blair."

There was still a pause. John tried again.

"Dic te verum."

A smile broke across this William Wallace's face. It was as wide as the crescent moon shining behind his left shoulder.

"Libertas optima rerum," came the response and both men clutched each other. "John, John Blair. So ye ended up a monk?"

"Aye, if no' a very guid yin. And ye've ended up....what?"

"Now that's a tale, but maybe a tale fur later. Introduce me tae yer friends."

"This is Alan Murray. He's a lay brother returning from Paris."

"Paris?" said Wallace. "Noo whit wis a lay brother dain' in Paris?"

"Learning music."

"Ye a singer?"

"Aye, a singer"

"Where are ye from?"

"Brechin."

He spat on the ground. Obviously the news of Balliol's behaviour at Brechin had sullied the name of the place.

"We'll maybe hear some sangs later. And?"

"This is Fraser Campbell," said John. "Also returned from Paris, but on the King's business."

You could feel the tension that suddenly descended. The hands of those within hearing distance move to their sword handles.

Conversations stopped. Wallace grew by a span. Fraser extended his hand. Wallace made no move.

"Aye," said Fraser "Sent oot on the King's business. Returned wi' ither business. We ha'e nae King. We will ha'e a King again."

Wallace's hand came out. "Amen to that," he said. "Come sit wi' us."

He led us near to the centre of the clearing where it seemed they had not long finished eating and the ground had been flattened. When we settled down, he turned to John.

"So what led you here?"

"Well, we heard that there was this outlaw roaming around Scotland creating havoc with the English. As the three o' us like travelling and creatin' havoc, we thought we might join him."

"And welcome ye are. Ah could dae wi' some prayers." He looked at Fraser. "But ah'm no' sure about diplomacy." And back to John. "John, I ha'e a mite o' a problem. The church is riddled wi' priests who think Edward's side is God's side. This maks ma Confession at times a little awkward. Ah'm thinkin' Ah could dae wi' ma ain priest. Frae henceforth yer Wallace's Priest."

And then me. "And ah've never had a singer before. But sure, there must be a first time for everything. Maybe singin's better than confessin'. Let's mak ye my singer. Frae henceforth yer Wallace's Singer."

CHAPTER TWENTY ONE

My First Battle

The following conversation was fairly brief. Wallace told us that he had had a recent run in with Sir Henry de Percy, whom Edward had appointed to be Warden of Galloway and Ayr. According to his story, Percy had around one hundred and eighty men, many mounted, in his baggage train, but Wallace's fifty men on foot routed them. The skirmish, he didn't call it a battle, resulted in much plunder, hence the amount of arms his men were bearing now.

He explained that this place where he was encamped was Keir Hill and that it was his intention to attack the Peel Tower just down the hill in Gargowans. The tower had been built to guard the ford over the River Forth and was occupied by English soldiers. It all sounded very casual as he outlined things, but, in my mind, he was going into battle. Ambushing a baggage train was one thing, but attacking a small castle was another.

"Will there be a fight?" I asked tentatively.

"No, no Singer. Them English will just walk oot an' say 'Help yersel'. Of course there'll be a fight. But wait till you see them Irish fightin'."

"The Irish?"

He waved the tree trunk that was pretending to be his arm in the direction of the men sitting and standing around. For a twenty four year old, he had a remarkable physique. "Ah have managed tae collect some Irish." I think he was about to explain further, but was interrupted by two men, who had ridden into the encampment, rushing up to him. Without any further conversation with us, he took them some way off, presumably so that we couldn't hear their conversation. Watching him, it was difficult to read any emotion on his face. He seemed to ask questions but neither frowned nor smiled at the answers. After a few minutes, he returned. The purpose in his step made us all stand.

"It seems there might be a bit of action the night," he said. "Ah had sent these two tae scout on the Tower. They tell me that the drawbridge is down and the guards asleep. Seems ah should take advantage o' the moment."

He turned away from us and started to talk to his men. The quiet voice that we had become used to took on another form. It might not have wakened the dead, but it must have disturbed them in their prolonged slumber.

"Men, Ah ken ye ha'e been marching the day. Ah know yer tired. Ah know ye a' want tae sleep. But the night's no' a night fur sleeping. The night's a night fur puttin' tae sleep. The Tower's no' guarded properly. We're gonnae take it the night. As them that occupy the Tower are uninvited guests in oor country, let them have a long sleep. But nae wimen or children hae to be touched. Touch them wi' wan finger and Ah'll remove that finger. Get ready tae leave. Don't pit oan tae much o' that armour. It'll slow ye down. There's good pickings tae be had in the Tower and probably mair armour as well. Efter tonight, we'll drink. Efter tonight, we'll sleep. But first, let's take back another part of our country. An' you Irish, we'd dae the same fur you. That place is no' just a Tower. It's a blemish. It's a blemish that says we live in an occupied land. Let us take it back for oorsels, for our countrymen, for Scotland."

A cheer just rose. I noticed one of the loudest to cheer was Fraser. While noticing that, I noticed also that I was cheering myself. For myself, for my countrymen, for Scotland.

He strode across to us. "Weel, friends, are ye fur some action?" But before any of us could reply, and in my case unsure what the reply would have been, he continued, "Naw, this isnae fur a priest. Maybe yer services'll be required at the end – or at their end. And Alan, ye can think o' some songs that might entertain us when a' this is done. Campbell?"

"Ah've no' aye been a diplomat, ye ken. Ah kin fight," replied Fraser. I could see a quick glance being exchanged between him and John.

"Gray," Wallace shouted across to another man, "Get them sorted oot wi' somethin' to fight wi." He turned back to us. "Ye may no' be fightin' but ye may ha'e tae defend yersels."

And so it was, in that simple way, we had been recruited into Wallace's army.

He shouted to his men to gather round. He explained that they would get as close to the Tower as possible without alerting those inside. It should be possible as the guards obviously weren't expecting anything and, although there was a crescent moon, there was also plenty of cloud. He told them to hold their positions under cover when they arrived and that, on a simple command of 'Men' from him, they should commence the attack. On entering the Tower, they should spread out and despatch the English troops before they could get organised.

A simple "All got it?" was followed by an equally simple "Let's move", and his men started off.

As the last of them disappeared into the forest, John turned to me and said "Our turn". And so we followed.

I'm not sure what I felt most. Excitement? Certainly. Fear? Absolutely. I hadn't had a sword strapped to my waist since before I left Scotland. If called to use it, my guess was I'd simply be delaying the inevitable. Better keep close to John then.

These thoughts were interrupted as I felt John pulling my sleeve and indicating that I should crouch down beside him. We had obviously reached the place and the troops were all also stopped and crouched, though I couldn't see many of them through the dense undergrowth.

John pulled my sleeve again and pointed towards the Tower. I could see Wallace shuffling forward. I could see he was making for a wooden door. None of his men moved. He was almost at the door. Then I saw his problem. There was a large iron bar across the door fixed to the side walls. He stood up quietly and his huge hands gripped the bar. Then he pulled.

The air was split with his accompanying scream, but the iron bar came away from its fixings. It actually looked as if part of the wall on each side of the door had also come away with the strength of his pulling. His scream ended and all that could be heard was his shout, 'Men'.

The single scream was replaced with the screams of sixty and his men moved from crouching to charging.

My first battle had begun.

CHAPTER TWENTY TWO

The Aftermath of Battle

While his men were running towards him, I saw Wallace kick down the wooden door, but that was all I saw of my first battle. John and I stayed where we were and only heard the sounds of the struggle. It was only after it was all over that I was able to piece together what had happened.

The noise of Wallace breaking down the door had woken the watchman. He attacked Wallace with his mace, but Wallace grabbed it out of his hand and used it to silence him forever. By this time the English soldiers had woken up, but also by this time the rest of Wallace's men had arrived. The Captain of the guard, Wallace found out afterwards, was one Captain Thirlwall. Wallace used the same mace to dispatch him. His men saw to the other twenty two English soldiers. It took John some time to carry out his priestly duties. But, just as Wallace had commanded, no women or children were harmed. They were simply ejected from the Tower.

It was the sight of them leaving that suggested to John and myself that the fighting must be over. We headed towards the Peel Tower cautiously, albeit we had the feeling in our bones that Wallace's attack had been successful.

When we arrived, his men were already working out the amount of the spoils. It was obvious that the wine wasn't going anywhere. It was for immediate consumption. A couple of hours ago this strange little army might have been tired, but there was no sign of that now. With the wine, there was the food. With the food, there was the wine. With the wine, there was the carousing. With the carousing, there was the wine.

Wallace was enjoying it all as much as his men. It was the least that John and Fraser and myself could do, but to join in. Fraser seemed in his element. He was obviously happier with the fighting than with the talking. We were a happy band that night and, as we collapsed at different times to sleep, we were a happier band. Indeed the provisions in the Tower were so plentiful, we stayed there for four days.

It was on the second evening, as we were settled in the Hall, that Wallace called me forward.

"Alan," he said, "It must be time for one of your songs. There's nae point in ha'eing a personal minstrel if he doesnae dae some minstrellin'."

It had been ages since I had sung, so I wasn't sure what state my voice would be in, but it would have seemed churlish to make excuses. So I sang. One of the tunes I had learned in Paris, but with my own words that I had been working on when we were passing the time in Amsteldam. Obviously I could only sing the one line of music. There was none of the part singing I had learned when I was away. But my audience was quiet for a bunch of soldiers. Though some, I heard, started to try to hum the tune. I think it was successful. When I had finished, Wallace raised his tankard, saying:

"Ye have a fine voice, Alan – a very fine voice. From henceforth ah ha'e decided that you shall sing efter every wan o' ma victories." And there were cheers.

I said that we stayed at the Tower for four days, but it wasn't all eating and drinking. While we got to know Wallace's men, we also used to find time for ourselves. It was Fraser who planned it. He said that if we were to stay with Wallace's force, then there was no way we could avoid having to fight eventually. So, out of sight of the rest, he would make us practice with our swords.

It didn't take John long to show how skilful he was. He said he had just been out of practice. What kind of life had this priest had? Taking arms is not the same as taking Mass. I was slower. But I had a good teacher in Fraser. I was mastering the slash and the parries.

"Ye'll dae fine," said Fraser, "But ye'll need tae strengthen that airm." And I knew he was right. I just didn't have the same power as the rest of them. Right, if I can get my voice in shape, I can get my right arm in shape. And so I started my exercises – those for my voice (for I didn't know how soon the next victory would be) and those for my arm.

But the time had come for Wallace to move on and move on with his accumulated plunder. There was no way he could leave any of his men behind to look after the Peel Tower, so, to prevent it falling back into English hands, he torched it.

Wallace didn't share his plans with us. Indeed, I am unsure if at that time he had a plan. For he could have forded the River Forth where we were at Gargowans, instead we skirted Stirling and followed the river until arriving opposite Kincardine. Here he intended to cross.

Kincardine is close to Cuilross. I could go back there. But it is also very close to Faukirk. That meant I was very close to Meg.

Oh, I wanted to stay with Wallace. He was making a difference. Yes, he was making enemies, but he was also making a new Scotland, our Scotland. But I was very close to Meg.

I spoke to John about my leaving our new band of friends.

"Leave if ye must, but no lassie's mair important than whit we're dain'."

"But I can't be as close and not try to find her," I replied.

"Look, ye dinna ken her name. Ye dinna ken whaur she stays. How ye gonna find her? Fur all ye ken she could be merrit noo and no' be thankful o' seein' ye."

It was that one sentence that made up my mind. I was very close to Meg. I would find her. Married or not. I went to Wallace and said that I had some business to attend to locally. That I would only be away for a short time. That I would attend to my business and catch up with him.

"Catch up wi' me? Ah'm no that sure where Ah'm goin'. But ah am sure ah'm no' leaving a trail behind me that some-one could follow. There's mair than you who'd like tae catch up wi' me. Why dae ye think we've been movin' at night an' no' durin' the day?"

I couldn't deny the truth of what he said. I didn't want to leave him but I had to find Meg. Eventually it was John who came up with something of a solution. Wherever Wallace went, John would find a church or a priory or an Abbey and he would talk to the priest there. He would tell them that he was expecting a lay brother to follow behind him with instructions from a Bishop and ask them to let him (me) know that John had been there. That way there would be a trail to follow without any linkage to Wallace.

Wallace agreed, though I sensed a little reluctantly. I guessed he wasn't used to trusting anyone but himself and he had only known us for a short time.

"So what's this 'business' that ye ha'e tae attend to?"

Before I could reply, or maybe because I took some moments to compose my reply, John stepped in.

"It's a lassie."

"A lassie," repeated Wallace. "An' whit makes a man gang oot o' his way fur a lassie?"

A difficult question to answer. But not for John.

"He's in love wi' her."

"Love is it. Well, my singer, you go chase yer love. An' ah'll chase mine. Whit ah do is for ma love o' ma country. When ma country is free again with a rightful King, ah'll start chasin' love. Go, Alan. Sing her love sangs. But come ye back fur ma victory sangs."

With that, I left them and headed for Faukirk. I was very close to Meg.

CHAPTER TWENTY THREE

Finding Meg

It was a short ride which took me to Faukirk.

It was a small town with its houses stretching in small streets from its Church. The Church was important, as the priests there owned the land round about. As I rode in, it seemed fairly quiet with people going about their chores.

I found lodgings with stabling and started thinking of how I would find Meg the next day. I didn't have much to go on. Her name was Meg and she sold nails. How many Megs who sold nails could there be? I would simply ask people in the streets, get directions to where she lived and go and meet her. And she said we should meet at the kirk. Then people at the kirk must know her. Simple.

Wrong. The next morning I set about asking people. No-one seemed to have heard of her. I tried describing her. But no such goddess seemed to walk the streets of this town. I asked where I could purchase nails. But no-one seemed to use nails in this town.

I tried the kirk. I stopped a priest and began the same series of questions. But he had never heard of her. He at least had a suggestion. Why don't I go to the Thanes House to the west of the town and ask there. One Sir John de Calentir was trying to get a register together of local households. I thanked him and rode out following his directions. I met a Steward at the House but, without a family name, he was unable to help. In any case, this register was only to contain the names of those who owed taxes to Sir John. A day in a small town and I can't find her. Where next, what next?

What was next was the same thing next day. With the same lack of success. All this time I had dreamed of Meg. All this time I had dreamed of being in this town and meeting her. Two days in a small town and I can't find her. Where next, what next?

What was next was to leave here and find Wallace and his men again. Hopefully with more success than I had in finding Meg. The next day I started my journey north. The obvious starting point was to follow Wallace and cross the Forth at Kincardine. When you cross the river, you have two choices – to head directly north or to go east first. If you go east, it is only a short ride to Cuilross where John and I had stayed at the Abbey. Where I had met Meg. Where did you go to Meg?

It was my reckoning that Blair would have persuaded Wallace to head in that direction given he could find lodgings for Wallace and himself and stood a reasonable chance of getting provisions for the rest of the men. I headed east.

Riding into Cuilross was a curious feeling. For all that had happened to me, nothing had happened to it. And the feeling was even greater when I approached the Abbey and the first person I met was Father Ambrose.

"Father," I shouted. He looked up, still holding one of his gardening tools. After all this time he didn't recognise me.

Then. "I'm sorry I don't have enough time to hear your Confession. You've been away so long it might take days to hear of all your sins." And he started to laugh. I dismounted and we hugged like old friends.

"You ready for some food – with salt," he asked.

"Yes, Father, I'm ready for some food. And one of my sins is that I'm used to having salt now."

"No sin, Alan. A Blessing."

As it wasn't time for the others to eat, we ate alone. But still in silence. Then , after our meal, Father Ambrose started the conversation with:

"A friend of yours passed by the other day. I think he expected you to be following him."

"John?"

"Aye, John Blair."

"Did he leave a message for me?"

"Aye, he did." But there was nothing more forthcoming.

"And his message was?"

"Follow the path of St Serf."

"Follow the path of St Serf?"

"Aye."

St. Serf? I remembered the name, but…. Of course, Meg had told me he had founded this village and that he had brought up St Kentigern.

"But St Serf's path is here. This is the village he started."

"That is true and it is where he is buried. But his path led further north. He began a Priory on an island on Loch Leven. The island is called St Serf's Inch."

"Then I should follow John there?

"Perhaps. But I'm not sure if it's a likely place for the sixty men and that friend of his to end up."

"Then what other path?"

"He also started a church at Dunnyne. They say he slew a dragon there with his staff."

"Not a mace?"

"What?"

"No matter." I decided that recounting Wallace's exploits might not place us in the best light. "How do I get to Dunnyne?"

"Make for Dunfermline. Stay at the Abbey. They will be able to tell you the road to take from there."

"Father, I am most grateful. Next time I visit, I promise to stay longer."

"I'm an old man. These lengthy Confessions are too tiring." And the smile that was playing around his lips vanished. He held my arms in his hands.

"Alan, you're a good man. John's a good man. These four friends he had with him are good men. Go, slay your dragon."

CHAPTER TWENTY FOUR

Following the Clues

Four friends? So where were the sixty? And where was Wallace? If he had been one of the four, at his height, Father Ambrose would have mentioned him. And yet, John's message was clear.

Had there been a problem? Had they encountered some English troops and had to split up? Had they fallen out?

I had little choice. Not knowing what had happened to the others, I could only follow John's messages. And so it was to Dunfermline.

After making myself known, I was shown the new Chapel they had built. Impatient as I was for the directions I needed, I had to wait until they showed me the new resting place of Queen Margaret, a resting place, they thought, suitable for a Saint. But eventually, after showing as much interest as I could, they proved Father Ambrose right. I was told the roads to follow to reach Dunnyne. So - hence to Dunnyne.

The church there was impressive with a large tower. Not so imposing as those I saw in France, but for a small Scottish village it was remarkable. I introduced myself to the Priest. Without any concerns now about the welfare of Wallace's men, I was quite direct and said I was trying to catch up with a monk who might have passed this way. He confirmed that one such had passed through a couple of days earlier.

"And did he leave a message?"

"He did. Come inside. I wrote it down. My memory is not so good nowadays."

Inside, you could see the church had only been built fairly recently. Indeed some parts had still to be completed. The priest produced a small piece of vellum and showed me what he had written. His script was beautiful, more fitting to an important manuscript than a mere message from a monk to a brother. Beautiful, but difficult to decipher. He read it for me.

"A mere lay brother also is an Abbot. From south to north."

I read it again, the words this time being quite clear. And I read it again. I understood the words, but it made no sense.

"Do you understand this?" I asked.

"No," came the reply, "That's why I thought it better to write it down."

"What kind of message is it that can't be understood?"

"The kind of message that shouldn't be shared or, if it is, only has meaning to the right person. Let me pour you some ale while you ponder. What is your name?"

"Alan."

"Come, Alan. Let us sit and sip."

We went into a small room behind the altar and he poured some ale. I sipped and pondered. I wondered if this message had any relevance to the previous one.

"St Serf came from the south," I stated.

"He did. From Rome, from Gaul, from Cuilross. All journeys from the south. But then he died here and was taken back south to Cuilross."

We both sipped and pondered.

"Perhaps the most obvious starting place is that you're a lay brother," he ventured.

"Yes, but not an Abbot. Nor likely to be one. He says " also is'."

"So are we trying to think of a present day Abbot?" At least it felt that he was trying to help.

"Well, it says 'Is'. Could be. I don't know. Could be anything."

"I wonder." This might be an advance. His pondering was turning into wondering. I thought better than to interrupt. "You said your name was Alan?"

"That's right."

"There was an Abbot called Alan. Cistercian."

"Near here," I asked.

"Balmerino. Not too far. He founded an Abbey there."

"And 'from south to north'?"

"Well, he came from Melrose Abbey about fifty years ago."

"That's from south to north."

"He came with twelve brothers seemingly. Yes, Abbot Alan."

"I think that must be it. How do I get to this Balmero?"

"Balmerino. Come, I'll show you."

And so my travels continued to this Balmerino. It was a handsome red sandstone building. But there wasn't much around it. There was a separate house which I assumed was the lodgings of the Abbot, an Abbot whose name I did not know. For although news of the founding Abbot – Alan – seemed well known, the current one had no such distinction. As I headed towards the house, a hooded monk came towards me and hailed me.

"Well, is this the lay brother who's following the monk?"

"Aye. I am."

"Well, the message is – *Follow the music."* He didn't seem to think an introduction was necessary, but I took him to be the Abbot.

"Follow the music," I repeated.

"Well, it seemed a bit mysterious to me, so later on that night, when your John Blair had had an ample sufficiency of wine, I asked him what it meant. All he could say was 'Guido, Guido'. Then 'Pish'."

My mind went back to Friar William and his endless story about Guido being the first man to find a way of writing down music. I must have told the story to John, though I couldn't remember when.

"Well," I said echoing his habit of speech, " Guido was from Arezzo. I'm not sure if he wanted me to follow the music there."

"Well, there was another Guido. He was the Prior of Kelso but he came up here and founded an Abbey at Lindores over a hundred years ago. Perhaps that was the Guido he meant?"

"How far is Lindores Abbey?"

"Well, I would think not more than half a day's ride. Would you like some sustenance before your journey?"

"Thank you, Father, no. I'll ride on and hope to catch up with him. And thank you for your help."

He gave me some directions to follow and I was quickly on my way. But as I turned my horse - not a Meg or a Henry - to leave, I heard, or at least I thought I heard, my unnamed monk mutter, "Well, pish."

CHAPTER TWENTY FIVE

Back with Wallace

It took me less than half a day to reach the Abbey at Lindores. Or at least to reach sight of the Abbey. It was another imposing building. I stopped for a minute to take in the view. I was about to ride off, when a voice emerged from the woods beside me.

"Ye took yer time." And John came riding out of the thicket.

"I might have been quicker if I hadn't to work out where the hell you were."

"Alan, Alan, profanity!"

"That's rich coming from you." But by this time we were engaged in some form of a hug of greeting. Not an easy act to achieve when both riders were still on horseback. "Are you with Wallace?"

"Naw. He's further oan. Past St John's Town."

"You waited for me here?"

"Ah came back here tae wait fur ye. Ah didnae want ye tae be ridin' into St John's Town. Full o' English. We'll stay at this Abbey the night and ride tae where he's camped the morrow. It's aboot a day's ride away if we avoid the toon."

We set off in the morning. We had shared stories of his journey round the coast to Lindores Abbey and of my journey following him. The more I heard, the more I knew this Scotland was not a safe country at this time. Almost to prove it, we gave St John's Town a wide berth, so it took us a fair time to reach Methven and the woods where Wallace and his men were encamped.

We paused around the outskirts of the woods as John was unsure as to exactly Wallace was. After a short time, we heard the horn that Wallace had taken to using to summon his men. By following the sound, we were able to join forces again.

"Weel, ma singer," he greeted me. "We'll need a sang the night."

"Another victory?"

"Aye, sort of. Make yersels at home. It might no' be like the standard o' a castle but we ha'e plenty o' food." And off he marched to deal with some other business in the camp.

As I turned, John was already pouring some wine form a pitcher. "Pish," he said, "But no' bad pish." I joined him only too grateful to wash some of the journey out of my mouth.

It was later that night that I learned of the 'sort of' victory. Apparently Wallace's journey to this wood, taking the more northernly route passed the River Teith and Strathearn, had involved taking on and killing any rogue English troops that had passed their way. He told the story of meeting five of them at Blackford. As was their way, after a skirmish, all five were killed. But, rather than advertise their presence, they hid the bodied before recommencing their journey to Doune. Wallace didn't embellish his stories. Indeed, I got the feeling that he didn't actually enjoy telling them. Rather that it was what had to be done and it was done.

It was getting dark as we sat around the fire. It was then Wallace announced that he was going into St John's Town the next day. Kerly, an old ally of Wallace's, remonstrated with him telling him that the Town was full of English, that he would likely get caught and that, if that were the case, everything they had done to this point would have been for naught. Wallace simply laughed.

"Ah'm no' goin' in annoucin' masel. Ah'll be discreet. Ah just want tae see whit's goin' oan."

It was John who rejoined with:

"Discreet ye may try tae be, but at your height Ah think ye might be noticed. And frae noticin' it willnae tak' them lang tae reach notoriety."

Wallace thought for all of three seconds, then asked:

"Where dae they ha'e big men?"

Steven, an Irishman in our group, contributed, "Sure, they men down near England. Many a big man there."

"Yer right, Steven. The men frae the borders see the clouds before most. So, I'll be frae Ettrick Forest." He threw a look at Kerly.

"Nae need tae look at me like that. Ye can be frae Ettrick if ye like. Jist mak sure yer nae frae Crugilton. Ma place widnae ha'e ye."

“Och, you people frae the borders not only see the clouds, ye’ve got yer heids in them. Noo, Ah’ll ha’e tae ha’e a name.”

“Why no’ choose one of your old King’s names. Then you can ride in pretending you’re the king.” It was Steven again.

“No’ a bad idea. Which wan? Malcolm. He wis known as The Great Chief.”

Kerly joined in this time with:

“Aye, but he wis also known as Virgo – The Maiden.”

If there had been any English troops around at that moment, I think we would all have perished. For the sound of our laughter must have carried for miles – led, I am happy to report, by Wallace himself. When he had composed himself a little, Wallace manage to splutter:

“As The Maiden, ah guess ma Great Chief is intact. Was it no’ Malcolm wha had that set to wi’ some six earls in St John’s Town?”

Without really answering the question, John came in with, “He wisnae a’ bad. Founded the Abbey for the Cistercians at Couper Angus.”

“There, ye see, ma Great Chief isnae a’ bad. Ah will therefore be proud tae be his son. Malcolmson. An’ ma known name?”

It was Kerly again. “Weel, as yer still The Maiden, how about Will? Tae show yer will power?”

More laughter. And more wine. Eventually, without the laughter and in a quite sober voice, Wallace declared;

“Guid. The morrow we go intae Toon. Kerly you’re wi’ me. Steven, you tak charge here. Kerly, pick anither five men tae come wi’ us. You twa,” he looked at John and me, “Get some ither claithes. You’re in the pairty too. Ah might be a maiden but ah’m no’ goin around wi’ men o’ the cloth. Should be interestin’, this Will Malcolmson gaein tae St John’s Toon. Should be very interestin’”

CHAPTER TWENTY SIX

Surveying the Town

We headed off the next morning as planned. For all I was quite used to wearing street clothes, the ones I was given were rough and not very comfortable. We bore no arms on Wallace's instructions. But the real sight was John Blair. I had never seen him other than in his habit and, even sitting astride his horse, I have never seen anyone look more uncomfortable.

Wallace signalled us to stop at an inn just outside of the town. As he dismounted, we all followed suit. He thought it inadvisable that a party of eight should ride in together. We might attract some unwanted attention. It was his plan that we should walk in in groups. If we should get separated, we should meet each other outside the Kirk of the Holy Cross. To this John somewhat needlessly added;

"Mair Dunfermline monks."

We tied up the horses, having given the innkeeper the wherewithal to watch over them, and started walking into town. The groups seemed to form naturally and I ended up walking with John.

The town was a busy place. Traders were going about their business. A smell of cooking everywhere, combined with less odorous smells. Oh, for the paving stones of Paris! Still, it was a busy place with a lot going on. I wondered if it was the type of place Meg would have liked. Plenty of English troops around, though the locals didn't seem perturbed by them. I guess they had just got used to them being around. Not sure how comfortable I'd be rubbing shoulders every day with armed troops proudly bearing Edward's emblem on their tunics. Not sure if I was comfortable at all just being near them at that moment.

John pointed forward. It was Wallace just entering an ale house just ahead. We walked on past and sat on a mounting block where we could still see the shop. Wallace emerged with a tankard of ale and what we took to be the owner of the ale house but, as much as we tried, we could only hear parts of their conversation.

John nudged me. "Hear that?" I shook my head. "He said 'Ah'm lookin' fur work'." By this time the innkeeper, if that's what he was, had scuttled off leaving Wallace standing outside with his tankard. His eyes were looking round establishing where each of us had chosen to stop. He was also checking that our various presences weren't attracting any attention. He must have been satisfied as he signalled across to us to join him.

We were unpractised in the art of not making ourselves look conspicuous, so I guess our deliberate amble over to his table probably looked peculiar in its slow exaggeration, had anyone been paying particular attention. But the walk was a mere rehearsal for the exaggeration of the greeting. We hugged more than could be supposed at the returning of the Prodigal Son. And we sat down beside him as he indicated. John, casually, lifted his feet up and placed them on the barrel that was substituting for a table. To emphasise the camaraderie between them and to give an even greater air of casualness, John lifted Wallace's tankard and helped himself to a mouthful.

"Pish," he said. This was not acting of the highest order.

"Ye seen how many troops are around?" asked Wallace.

"Aye. Mair Edward's men here than onywhere else ah reckon," offered John.

"We'll no' be takin' this toon, ah fear. No' today anyway." And Wallace's eyes continued to survey the area around him. "Kerly's makin' friends," he observed.

Sure enough, across the road, Kerly and two others seemed to be in deep conversation.

"Ah'll be trustin' he's keeping' his ain mooth shut," Wallace continued, his eyes not averting from following Kerly.

As much to join in the conversation as to add anything of substance, I added, "He doesn't usually speak a lot."

Wallace turned to face me. I could almost hear his question forming. 'And how do you know that being with us such a little time?' But the unspoken question was interrupted by the return of the innkeeper, accompanied by another gentleman. The gentleman, for so he was dressed, stretched out his hand.

"Mercer, " he said, offering his name.

"Malcolmson," Wallace replied without a pause.

"I'm Provost here in St John's Town. We like to welcome strangers who come on business."

"And nae doubt gi'e a different kind o' welcome tae those wi' dubious business." Wallace's smile stretched across his whole face. How could one so open be on 'dubious business'?

"Aye, that as well. And your business is?"

"Ah've come frae Ettrick Forest. Ah was thinkin' a could find a better livin' and a better dwellin' here in the auld capital of oor country."

"Good, good. We will wish you well in that endeavour. Have you heard about an outlaw Wallace in your travels?"

Not a muscle moved on Wallace's face. If anything his smile broadened, as he replied:

"Ah've heard speak o' the man, but tidings of him can I tell you none."

"Good, good. You would report to us anything you heard or saw?"

"Mercer, if ah came across a true outlaw ah'd make it ma business tae deal wi' him first and then report ma actions tae them in authority."

"Good, good man. Well, as I say, we wish you well in your endeavours. Good, good. God be with you." And Mercer turned and walked away, ignoring the innkeeper as he exited. The innkeeper, presumably now assured his customer was bona fide, turned his mind to trade.

"Ye'll be wantin' mair ale?"

"Naw. We'll stairt lookin' for work and lodgings. But ah'm sure we'll be back tae grace yer premises again." He pulled out some coins and passed them to the innkeeper. By the look on the recipient's face, the sillar was more than adequate for one tankard of ale. Wallace looked at the two of us.

"Weel, noo that we've renewed oor friendship, will ye no' walk wi' me?" His smile was now one of plotter to fellow plotter.

"We surely will, " said John answering for both of us. But before he started that walk, he lifted the tankard and drained its contents. "Pish."

And so we started walking back to where we had tethered our horses. Wallace gave a discreet signal with an imperceptible nod of his head to the other two groups. One group immediately started following, but Kerly's hand gesture indicated that he acknowledged the summons but would follow in his own time.

"So, whit's he up tae?" said Wallace. "Yon Kerly's either plannin' somethin' or findin' oot somethin'. He'd better no' be thinkin' ah'm daen' anythin'. There's too mony wearin' Edward's airms fur me tae be interested in this toon."

"Maybe he's just made some new friends. Maybe he's just asking what's been going on. Maybe…"

"Pish" was Wallace's laconic reply. Nothing like extending your vocabulary from a holy man!

CHAPTER TWENTY SEVEN

Preparations for Another Battle

So we left, walking from one innkeeper to another, to collect our horses. Wallace's eyes were constantly looking round to see if the recalcitrant Kerly was anywhere to be seen. But so far, no sign. We met up with our horses again and sat and waited. There wasn't a lot of talking as Wallace was plainly disturbed by the wait, or, at least, the possible cause of the wait.

After a little while – well, it seemed quite a long while – Kerly could be seen approaching, running vey fast. He had hardly reached us when he started to blurt out:

"Sorry an' that. But wait till ah tell ye whit ah've fun oot."

Wallace rose and raised his hand. "Wheesht, man," and pointing, "that barley has ears. Whatever it is, it can wait till we're back in camp."

We rode back. Though this time Wallace seemed to suggest some urgency as our return journey was done at the gallop as opposed to the contained trot of our journey to town. As we entered the woods, Wallace slowed to a walk. Presumably so that his posted sentries could identify who this party was and allow safe entry. However his dismount, and the throwing of his reins to others to look after his horse, suggested that impatience still flowed through his veins.

"Well?" was the question as Kerly caught up with him. This time a laconic question.

"Ah wis speaking tae one o' the merchants in town. He wis so pleased wi' things, he couldna keep his mouth shut. He jist went oan an' oan. Ah could hardly get a word in. Ah tell ye, things couldna hiv been better fur him."

Wallace obviously wished that his laconic manner was infectious. "Get oan wi' it. Whit did ye find oot?"

"He had to provision a small force which wis due tae arrive at Kinclaven Castle. Made a lot o' sillar."

"Ah'm no' interested in how much sillar the man was makin'. How big is the 'small force'?"

"He said he had to make provision for one hundred."

The pause suggested Wallace was weighing up the odds. His sixty against one hundred? "Do ye ken who's leading them?"

"He said his Bill would be paid by Sir James Butler."

"That old English bastard." No pause this time. The name had obviously triggered decision.

Wallace blew his horn to summon his men. The camp was fairly rambling and with some of his men on guard duty and others foraging in the woods, this was the quickest way of getting everybody together. They all knew, at the sound of the horn, to gather together. And so it was, he blew his horn. And so it was, they gathered together.

"Men," Wallace started, "We have just returned from St John's Town. The place is hoachin' wi' English troops. Oor auld capitol will ha'e tae wait awhile afore we kin mak it a Scottish toon again. But Ah widnae deny ye a fight. Ah widnae deny ye some spoils. Ah widnae deny ye the chance tae strike at them English again. We ha'e fun some English. Are ye up fur the fight?"

The shout that went up was not a unified 'Aye', but, by its nature, it surely indicated they were up for the fight. Indeed, the Irish voices seemed more vociferous than those of the Scots.

"Then, close doon the camp. When we return, it will be wi' plenty. Get yersels ready. Mak yer weapons sharp. Mak every blow count fur Scotland."

As the men dispersed to do his bidding, he turned back to us. "Kerly, ride oan ahead an' look fur a place where we can surprise them. The castle's defences are too much fur us. We must get them afore they reach it. We need a place whaur we kin hide and surprise them." And Kerly left. He turned to Fraser. "Hiv ye goat this man up tae speed wi' a sword?" He was pointing at me.

"Aye," said Fraser, "He kin match any o' your men noo."

I was ready to disagree but didn't have the chance.

"Then ye'll ride wi' us, singer. An' while yer fightin' ye kin be composin'. Campbell, when Kerly has fun us a spot, we'll split up the men. Ye'll command wan lot and ah'll be in charge o' the other.

John, ye'll come tae. We'll save yer prayers fur efterwards. But nae prayin' while yer fightin'."

With that, he simply got up and left us to get himself ready. It was Fraser who spoke first:

"Weel, seems like we ha'e goat a fight oan oor hands. Come oan, Alan, let's see whit you kin dae wi' all that practisin'."

And so, it was into battle. But this time, for me, it was to be as a fighter, not an observer. The other two had already started moving.

"Come oan," said John. He stood looking at me. Then simply said, "Bonny fechter."

CHAPTER TWENTY EIGHT

Kinclaven Castle

Kerly had done his job. He had found a place just before Kinclaven Castle. But, while within sight of the Castle, he had chosen a hollow with plenty of trees where our men could be hidden. I saw Wallace congratulate Kerly on his choice and saw him calling over Fraser Campbell.

"We'll split the men up. Ye can tak that side ower there. Keep weel hidden. On ma signal, we baith come oot wi' oor men and stand across the road. We'll let them see us, but we'll just stand. Then, at the last moment, when ah tell ye, we'll split tae each side an' then attack their horses. Keep the men weel hidden and quiet or the whole thing willnae work." And then, addressing all the men, "Split up on either side and get yersels hidden. Those o' ye wi' horses, get them tied up way back whaur they can eat." His last words to Fraser were, "The last thing we need is them horses whinnying and gi'en us away. Mind, dinnae move tae a gie the whistle." His last words to me were, "Put that sword to guid use, singer."

Fraser grabbed me by the elbow and propelled me into the heavy undergrowth. He almost threw me behind a tree and then made a survey of the men ensuring that no part of them could be seen and reminding them of the need for silence. When he returned, he took up a position lying beside me. In a hushed voice, he said,"Ye see them sword lessons. Ye'll no' need them at first. Aim for the horses bellies. When they canna ride, they'll fight. That's when tae use whit ye've learned." I was unsure what a liked least – the prospect of harming, indeed killing, horses or the prospect of harming, indeed killing, men. I was as unsure as that first time I was given a sword all that time ago in Brechin.

We hunckered down and waited. From where I was I could see no sign of the other men, nor hear a sound.

It wasn't too long before I felt a nudge on my arm from Fraser. He tapped his ear with his finger. Sure enough, I could hear the sound of horses. It was almost as if the sound came through the ground rather than through the air. I felt Fraser's body tense ready to dart forward onto the road.

The beat of the horses' hooves got nearer. Very close. But still no whistle.

Then three horsemen rode passed.

Wallace must have guessed that there would be outriders to make sure the road was safe for the main group of troops. The sound of the horses began to fade away. Still there was no sound from the men in hiding. I was impressed with their discipline.

If I could hear three horsemen through the ground, then the next sound was as if the core of the earth was rumbling. This was the sound of many horses. A sound that was echoing round the hollow we were in and vibrating through the earth.

Then Wallace whistled.

The sound level increased as the yells of Wallace's men joined that of the approaching horses. They scurried from their hiding places and formed a barrier across the road. Then they fell silent. I was with them, making the same noise and falling equally silent. We watched the approaching troops of Butler. I saw them lowering their lances. Still there was no signal from Wallace. Still we didn't move.

Then, at what seemed like the last moment, Wallace shouted to clear. We fell to either side of the road just before their lances could reach us. And then the carnage began.

Accompanied by more yells, we fell into the horses, slashing at legs and thrusting at bellies. The English troops had no defence when their horses fell. Their lances were useless against our swords and they had no arms for hand to hand combat. I hacked with the best of them, caught up with the intensity of the battle.

Beside me, all of a sudden, was Kerly. He wasn't using a sword. He was using a mace which, although I had little time to see it, looked remarkably like the one Wallace had gained at the Peel Tower at Gargowans. And then I saw Wallace.

He had caught up with Sir James Butler himself. It was an unequal fight as our young, muscular leader dispatched the old English warrior.

It was as if that was the signal. The English troops, for all their numerical supremacy, were already in disarray, but, seeing their leader downed, they started fleeing to Kinclaven Castle. We followed stepping over dead and dying horses and, I'm afraid, dead and dying men.

When we reached the drawbridge of the castle, it offered no defence as, by this time, the fleeing and the following were one mass and both entered together. The destruction continued. It took some hours before all the enemy were accounted for. At the end of the day, with Wallace sparing the lives of the women and children – and, at John's bidding, two priests - the castle was ours and the task of clearing up began.

John's work was not done. With some sixteen bodies lying dead on the road and another eighty or so around the castle, he worked his way round saying his prayers.

On Wallace's orders, provisions and strong boxes and anything else of value was assembled by the drawbridge. The horses were brought back and added to by the remaining English horses. They were loaded up like pack horses to return to Methven Wood. The castle itself was set alight by Wallace. With such few troops, he couldn't afford to leave a detachment there to guard it.

I was one of the last to leave. The castle by this time was well ablaze and it stood out like a beacon against the night sky. A beacon of destruction? Or a beacon of freedom?

As I rode back, my blood-stained sword in its scabbard, the exhilaration of the battle had passed. The blood that stained my clothing stained my heart. All these lives lost. But they shouldn't have been here. This was our land. They were draining our blood. And in my mind, still the picture of John going round the bodies – bodies of enemies, but souls to be sent to heaven.

But it had been a good day, a successful day. A day where Wallace's tactics had proven to be a match for the superior English force. A day where Wallace had few casualties. A day where Wallace, for his band of sixty, had only lost five men.

But it was not a night for singing.

CHAPTER TWENTY NINE

Methven Wood

I was lucky. There was no request for singing.

When we got back to the camp in Methven Wood, Wallace was to busy organising the booty they had collected. Provisions had to be stored. Wine stacked ready for use. And he ordered pits to be dug in order that the coin could be hidden until later. But in so organising, he was careful to make sure that each of his men got his own allocation of provisions and wine and coin. When the bounty is plentiful, the leader can be bountiful. With an admonition to his men, "Watch the drinkin' We're movin' early in the morn," he came over and joined us.

I greeted him with, "Successful day."

"Aye," he replied, "But it may no' be the morrow. Them women frae the castle will ha'e alerted the troops in the toon. And if they doubted them, they havnae far tae go to see the sky light up wi' the castle oan fire. They'll be here the morrow and in the kinda numbers ah widnae like tae contemplate. And fresh men. Ma men'll be tired."

"Should we no' just move on now?" It was John.

"Naw. There has tae be a wee bit celebration. It's no' every day ye defeat the English and take wan o' their castles. Or wan o' oor castles that they took. Naw. We'll move in the mornin'. God be with you this night." I was lucky. Singing was not mentioned.

When we arose in the morning, it became clear that Wallace had already used the early hours to scout and choose his defensive positions. He was already marshalling his men and taking them further into the dense forest. We simply followed. He showed them the clearing he had chosen and told them to cut down trees and use them tied to other trees to form walls which they should infill with thorns thus creating a kind of corral. He worked back from this point choosing places along the forest path where he could narrow the track with logs and branches so only allowing one horse to pass at a time. He would then leave some men at each of these wooden funnels. It wasn't too long before Wallace had everything in place. But in place for what?

"So what are ye expectin'?" It was John again.

"Ah'm expecting Butler's son. Nae son worth his salt just accepts his faither's death. He'll be comin' efter us. But he' ll come efter us wi' heavy horse. Ma plan is to get rid o' as mony o' them through this track wan at a time. The others we'll deal wi' when they reach the stockade. It's gonna be messy."

And messy it was. The first part of Wallace's plan worked well. Sir John – for that was the son's name –Butler did lead the attack. But, as Wallace had anticipated, his heavy horse couldn't manoeuvre well in the dense forest and, as they came to the narrow parts of the path Wallace had created, they were dispatched with some ease. I was glad not to be involved in this fighting. My stomach for killing horses had not got any stronger even though I could see how successful the ploy was. Indeed, the slaughtering of both men and horses reinforced Wallace's plan as they created more self-made barriers, impeding those coming behind and making the ambushing for Wallace's men easier.

Then there came a lull. Such horsemen as were still astride their horses retreated. A cry went up from the men, sensing they had achieved another victory. Then a horn sounded and the stentorian voice of Wallace could be heard:

"Men, this isnae it. They've no' run away. They'll be comin' back. The garrison at St John's Town is big. They willnae just ha'e sent a few efter us. There's mair tae come. Stay in yer places and await ma orders."

Once again he was right. The next thing to attack us wasn't horses but arrows. Butler had seen the destruction of his heavy horse and decided on another tactic. His archers were well spread out and their volleys were coming from different directions, but those that hit were causing lethal damage. Wallace was swift to acknowledge the threat. He called Fraser Campbell across:

"Get back to the stockade an' get the men frae there. Split them up into twa groups. Get each group tae circle round an' attack them archers frae either side. When ye get in close, the fightin' will be easy. They don't usually hiv ither weapons."

Fraser moved immediately.

"You, Singer, stay wi' me."

He grabbed our horses and we rode up the path to check on the various groups of men and assess what damage had been done. Thankfully very few were injured. He told them to hold their positions and await his next orders, then:

"Right, let's get intae a position whaur we can see how that Campbell's getting' oan wi' these archers."

We were just riding off when one of the arrows caught him on his neck just above his steel mail and he fell off his horse. He made an initial yell, but then stifled it, presumably not to let the men know he had been injured. But by his twisting movements on the ground I could see he was in a lot of pain.

"You all right?"

"Get this thing oot." The arrow was still protruding from the left hand side of his neck.

"What with?"

"Snap the bloody thing furst."

"Right. Right. Hold still."

I think he was in too much pain to notice my trembling hands. I took hold of the arrow shaft and broke it as close to the entry point as possible. This time he did yell. The arrow's point must have reached some bone.

"Noo, get it oot." His hands move from protecting the wound to his belt. From there he produced a knife. "Get it oot noo."

I took the knife and looked to see how I was going to remove the arrow point. It seemed quite deeply embedded. "This will hurt," I said, perhaps needlessly.

"Of course it'll hurt. Get oan wi' it."

I slid the knife in, following as close as I could to the metal. When I thought I had reached the tip, I turned the knife in the hope of dislodging it. It came away first time. Wallace's face was ashen white. I expected him to pass out any minute. But, for all the obvious pain incurred in releasing the arrow point, not a sound escaped from his clenched teeth. Then he inhaled three enormous deep breaths and sat up.

"Cut some o' ma shirt a wrap it up."

I cut my own sleeve off and wrapped it around his neck, pressing down with my hand in an attempt to stop the flow of blood. He started to rise.

"Don't get up. Sit there till I go and get help."

"Ye'll dae nae such thing. Get the horses an' help me up."

By the time I had brought over the horses, he had deemed my help unnecessary and had already risen to his feet,

"Now, help me up."

I helped him up onto his horse. "Narry a word," he commanded. I nodded, thinking it wouldn't take any word from me. He would never be able to ride with that pain and a crudely bandaged neck and shoulder. I guessed his men might realise there was something of a problem when they saw him falling off his mount. "Come oan. Let's see whit that Campbell fellow's up tae. Let's hope he's got the wan that did this tae me."

And he took off. And he rode off. And he didn't fall off.

CHAPTER THIRTY

No Retreat

He led us to a clearing in the forest with slight rise. From there we were able to see the fight between Fraser and the English bowmen. It looked much as Wallace predicted. The English archers were being dealt with at close quarters by Campbell and his men.

"Seems like thon Campbell's copin'. Ah didna doubt it. Still, jist as weel. There's only aboot twenty o' ma men hae bows and their no' very guid wi' them. Come oan, let's get back."

"Wait," I said. "What's that over there?"

There was a cloud of dust approaching. Wallace peered for a few seconds before announcing:

"Aye, that's just whit we need. Looks like they ca'ed up reinforcements. Must be near three hunner o' them. Must be bloody breedin' them in St John's Toon. Come oan."

As he jerked at the bridle of this horse, I could see the pain shooting through his body, but still he made no sound or no complaint. Nor did he take it gently. He put his horse to the gallop.

Back nearer the action, he sounded his horn again as a signal to his men to regroup. This time it took longer for the troops to assemble. Breaking off the skirmishes had to be completed without the danger of being followed. When most were back, he told them of the other troops that we had seen arriving. He said the numbers against us now were going to prove difficult. He ordered that we gathered our horses and our weapons so that we could move to another place in the forest which would be more advantageous to us in the forthcoming fight. He never said 'run from here'. He never said 'flee'. He never used the word 'retreat'. But we all knew that's what it was.

I looked around at the tired men, at the wounded men. They had been fighting all right. I felt guilty about my paltry contribution. They did as they had been bidden, but you could see that they had had enough. Their shoulders were down. They walked heavily.

There were no yells, no excitement, no jubilation. Indeed, there was virtually no conversation as they got their horses and weapons.

As soon as all were ready, Wallace led us off. We followed to this 'better defensive position'. I did not occur to any of us that Wallace had not scouted this area before and had no idea where he was leading us. We just followed, trusting on this man who had shown us how to fight our enemy. Campbell just followed trusting that the archers he had routed hadn't regrouped. I just followed, trusting that the wound to his neck would not incapacitate him further. John just followed, I think for the first real time, trusting in God.

I was riding alongside John Blair. I became conscious that he was muttering. It was indistinct and it took me some time to realise he was speaking in Latin. Eventually I worked it out. He was repeating, 'Deo Speramus, Deo Speramus.' In God we trust, in God we trust. Even as we rode, not in flight, not in retreat, through the forest I remembered another lay brother back in Brechin. His name was also Alan – Alan Lyon. He told me that his family's motto was "In Te Domine Speravi" – In thee Oh Lord have I put my trust. A strange time to remember that, but, under my breath, I also whispered "Deo Speramus". And Wallace.

But we came to doubt if that trust was misplaced.

We arrived at the River Tay. It was far too deep here to cross. On one side there was also a steep crag. There was no way this was the 'better defensive position', but he had little choice. This is where we had come to, this is where we must fight. Wallace called a halt and sat still for a little while before dismounting. Again I thought I could see a wince across his face as the shudder of his landing reached his neck. He looked around at this small party of men, most of whom were wounded and exhausted. He must have been thinking of Butler's troops plus the three hundred extra which by now must have joined them. We were badly outnumbered. This was surely the end.

He bent down and picked up a handful of earth.

"Men," he said, "this is ma earth. This is your earth. This is yer children's earth. Whit pairt o' this earth belongs tae them English? If it's theirs, gi'e it tae them. If it's no' theirs, then it's oors and it's worth fightin' fur. No' maybe fur oorsels, but frae oor children an' them that cam' efter us."

He let the earth fall through his fingers.

"Aye, we can be like the worms an' hide in it or we can be like men an' stand oan it. We can stand and fight oan it. Fur we're no' fightin' fur this wee bit forest, fur this wee bit land, this wee bit earth.

Wur fightin' fur oor country, oor land, oor heritage and, aye, oor children's heritage. On this earth we will fight. Some o' us may shed oor blood oan this earth. But ken what? That'll make it mair Scottish. That'll mak' it land that should ne'er feel an English boot. That'll mak' it oor land again.

Tae all o' ye, frae the bottom o' ma hairt, ah thank ye. Ah thank ye fur what ye hiv done fur Scotland. Today we might no' see independence, but each o' yer steps oan this earth has been pairt o' th journey. Step oot, wan mair time, fur yersels, fur yer children, fur Scotland."

For a second, the word 'Scotland' hung in the air. Then those tired men, those wounded men, those defeated men took up the cry together, echoing through the forest and reverberating off the earth: 'Scotland, Scotland.'

CHAPTER THIRTY ONE

Getting the Spoils

You could almost see his men become taller. They were ready to fight. I was ready to fight. And fight they did. And fight I did.

The English had broken up into separate parties to search the woods and flush out this 'outlaw'. In minutes after Wallace had addressed his troops, one of the search parties stumbled into us. They were the unfortunate ones. So fired up were Wallace's men, that every one of the English troops was slaughtered. But Wallace's men also sustained more casualties. It would not be possible to fight again when the main cohort of the English army arrived. He himself looked exhausted and, although he held his sword in his right arm, you could see the blood seeping through the bandage covering the wound on the left side of his neck. Wallace had no choice.

He turned to Fraser Campbell. "We'll ha'e tae move. There'll be nane o' us left standin' if we wait around here much longer."

"No' better tae hide? It'll be dark soon."

"Naw. There's too mony o' them. An' look at these men. They're exhausted. Time tae call a halt."

And call a halt he did. He told them all that we would mount up and ride out of the forest. Riding fast and riding together. If we met any of the English army, we would fight our way through, but only to make an escape, not to prolong the battle. When we were out of the forest, we would split up. We should all go back home. He would send messengers to tell us when and where to meet up again.

It was a quieter Wallace. It was only a couple of hours since he had made his rousing speech and here he was telling us all it was over. We should go home.

"And whaur's your hame?" John asked Wallace.

"Ah've no' decided. First thing is tae get oot o' here."

"Aye, but then ye'll need tae point that horse somewhere."

"John, John. Ye've known me lang enough. Ah'll dae aw right."

"Ye'll nae dae aw right if ye don't get that neck seen tae. And it's no' safe tae stay onywhere aroond here. Here's what we'll dae. Aye, we'll a' split up when we get oot o' here. But we'll a' head fur the Abbey of St Mary o' Stirling. It's jist outside o' Stirling. They're Augustinians there. They'll no' say onythin'. And they'll sort oot yer neck fur ye."

It was as if Wallace was grateful that someone else was making the decision for him. He didn't argue. He didn't ask any questions. He just said 'Aye', and with that turned to his men as if to give them his orders. But he stopped and turned back to us.

"Aye. But there's jist wan thing afore we go. You three." His decision-making had obviously returned. "See that stuff we buried from Kinclaven Castle. Noo it wad be a pity tae leave it jist buried in the groon'."

"Or the Scottish earth," said John. If Wallace understood what John was alluding to, he showed no signs of it.

"Aye. You three can go back an' get it. If yer stopped, ye stand a better chance of foolin' them than any o' the rest o' us. Jist get the gold and the coins. Leave the rest."

"Noo that's kind o' ye. Ah suppose it'll be aw right if we ha'e some o' that pish wine?" If Wallace understood John was joking, he showed no signs of it.

"Aye. An' we'll sort oot the sillar at the Abbey." And this time he did turn to the men and gave them the command to gather together and ride out.

It was much later before we found out that Sir John Butler had surrounded the forest with his troops and that Wallace and his men did have another fight on their hands before they burst through the encircling troops. But get through they did and scatter they did.

The three of us watched them go with mixed feelings. These were the men we had just finished fighting side by side with. We should be with them. But we understood Wallace's need for funds and the need to go back and get the hoard. But why us? This was a more dangerous task than the others had. They were riding out of the wood, we were riding deeper into it. They were escaping from the enemy, we were probably going to meet them. It was Fraser Campbell who broke into our thoughts.

"Maybe we should get rid o' oor weapons. Dinna think we should look like fightin' men."

"Right," said John, and started to hide his sword in the bushes. We both followed suit. "Now whit?"

"Noo we go an' get the stuff."

"An' ye ken the way back?"

"Aye. Ah'll find it."

"An' if we meet some o' they troops?"

"We'll say we're oot huntin'."

"Wi' oor bare hands?"

"Aye, weel. Maybe we're gang tae St John's Toon tae look fur work an' lodgings. Aye, that'll do."

"That'll do?"

"Aye. Look, we have a sayin' in oor family – do and hope. So let's get oan wi' it. Let's do it."

"Fraser, ye're some man. But do it we will. You can have the doing. Alan here can do the hopin'. An' ah'll dae the prayin'. An' ah've a funny feeling which wan o' us is the mair important."

And so we set off, but at least we set off with smiles on our faces.

CHAPTER THIRTY TWO

From Cambuskenneth to Dunipace

I'm not sure whether it was John's praying or my hoping, but God – or luck – was on our side. Fraser managed to lead us back to the former camp site and we encountered no English troops on the way. Occasionally we could hear their sound but we just stopped the horses and waited for the sounds to pass. We unearthed – with no joke from John -the stored goods, leaving the provisions and separating the gold, silver and coin. John did, however, sample some of the pish. Fraser and I declined, though, from sampling it before, it was particularly good pish.

What we now had to carry was too much to hide on our person so we made bags from the hessian to tie to our saddles.

"If we're stopped noo whit's the story?" John asked of Campbell.

"Wir lookin' fur particularly guid lodgings," he replied.

And so, in the morning, the three of us started on the road from Methven Wood to the Abbey at Cambuskenneth. Again we encountered no-one and our journey was without incident. We had to stop overnight so it wasn't until the next day we arrived at the Abbey.

There the news was not so good.

Yes, Wallace had reached the Abbey. But his journey had plenty of incident. After fighting their way out of the forest, Wallace had started off alone. As luck – or God – would have it, he came across Sir John Butler. The recognition on both sides resulted in a fight in which Butler came off worse. He grabbed Butler's horse and rode off with English troops following him. Eventually they caught him up and another fight ensued, this time Wallace dispatched twenty of the soldiers. He rode on but Butler's horse didn't have Wallace's resilience. It died of exhaustion at Blackford, leaving Wallace some fifteen miles of walking to reach the Abbey.

Then the news got worse.

Although he had reached the Abbey and told the monks of his journey, he had decided not to wait there. According to their story, they had pleaded with him, telling him his body needed a rest and time to recuperate, but to no avail. He left them. All he said was that if anybody should ask for him, the monks should say 'Uncle'.

He didn't head west (that's the direction from which he had come). He didn't head east (perhaps to Cuilross or Dunfermline). He headed south. And that meant crossing the River Forth. There is no ford at Cambuskenneth, so Wallace, weakened from his injury and exhausted from battle, swam the river, a river which is very wide at this point. The monks had watched him, fearing he wouldn't make it. But make it he did, as they saw him in the distance struggling to get up the bank on the far side

The three of us stood quietly absorbing the news the monks had told us. It was John who spoke first. "Uncle? Uncle. He has an uncle who's a priest at Dunipace."

"Dunipace? How far's that?" asked Fraser

"About half a day's ride," was the reply.

"Do you think that's what he meant?" I asked.

"Look," John replied, "We agreed tae meet here at the Abbey. He got here but he didna stay. Ma guess is that he kens how badly injured he is and that he needs a place tae take time an' get better. Stayin' here might put everyone else here at risk. So he heads for a safe place. His uncle's. No' mony people would ken he had an uncle in Dunipace, but he kent ah would. Ah hiv nae doubt that he's there."

"Then what the hell are we waitin' fur? Let's get the horses an' get goin'". Fraser was never one for inaction given the choice of doing something.

We crossed the Forth at Kincardine on our way to Dunipace. I couldn't help but remember the last time I had been here and my trip back into Faukirk to try to find Meg. As we headed towards Dunipace, so we got nearer to Faukirk. As we skirted round its edges, I so wanted to go into the town and try again. My heart told me my Meg was there. My head told me that she wasn't there last time. We rode on.

And then it dawned on me. After all this time thinking of her – on the boat to the Low Countries, in Paris, when I got home, when I went looking for her – she has become 'my' Meg. Now my heart and my head were together. If she was 'my' Meg, then she had to become my Meg. I had to find her. But first Wallace.

Dunipace is a small place and finding a priest is easy, so it didn't take us long to find Wallace. And we found him a sick man.

Yes, he had managed to cross the Forth, and, yes, he had managed to stagger on for a little while, but, by the time he reached the Torwood, he was completely exhausted. A widow woman had found him and tended his wounds. As she had three sons, she was able to give him fresh clothing. Two of her sons created a hidden den in the woods so that he could recover away from any prying eyes. The third son went on to Dunipace to tell Wallace's uncle that he was safe and would reach him soon.

But sick or not, he greeted us warmly and, as we shared a repast, it was good to see him eating. It might take some time before his massive frame was filled up again. But it seemed that a start was being made.

John, as might be guessed, had managed to get Wallace's uncle to open his supplies of wine and we sat by the fire if not content, then pleased we were all together again. The silence might just have been to share that moment of camaraderie or we might all have been awaiting John's verdict on the wine. But the silence was broken by Wallace.

"Ah'm leavin'."

"Yer in no state tae be goin' onywhere," Fraser said.

"Whaur ah am pits ithers in danger. There's been enough death with those around me. Ah canna endanger an old man like him." We knew he was thinking of his uncle, but, in the depths of his eyes, I thought he was still thinking of the men he had lost.

"Ye jist need a little time. Then ye'll be back oan the march. Ye'll ha'e an army again soon enough," said John.

"He thinks not," said Wallace with a nod indicating his priestly uncle who was not with us. "He thinks ah've lost ma men an' ah've lost everythin'. Noo's the time tae tell Edward that ah want tae make peace."

It was Fraser who started it. One of his largest laughs. John and I were soon to join in and then Wallace. Not one of us could imagine Wallace seeking peace with Edward. Not one of us who heard him talking about Scotland being free could imagine him seeking peace with Edward. Not one of us who had seen him fighting for the cause could imagine him seeking peace with Edward. And then the sound of our laughter got bigger. We all looked round to see who had enhanced the volume of our mirth. And there they stood: Kerly and Stephen, the Irishman.

The laughter moved to hugs and welcomes and cheers. It wasn't the meal, but you could almost see Wallace body get bigger. More supporters, more friends. As the various greetings died down and before they could tell their story of how they had found us, John was the first to react.

"This calls fur mair wine. Ah'll get some goblets." And so he departed with as much enthusiasm as he would if preparing for Mass.

Wallace brought them up to speed on his immediate plans which were to head to Dundaff, a fording place on the River Carron. It was quiet there and he had little chance of being found or of people turning him in. He would let Sir John Graeme know he was in the area, for those were his lands, and hope that that was all the protection he would need.

John returned and started pouring the wine for Kerly and Stephen. "Ye'll be needin' this," he said as he distributed it, meanwhile also replenishing our goblets. "Efter yer travellin'. It's guid stuff."

John's endorsement of the wine, unheard by any of us before, started Fraser off on another convulsion of laughter. The emotion being infectious, once again we all found ourselves laughing. Even John, though I'm unsure if he realised its source.

Kerly was the first to control himself enough to be able to speak.

"We're with ye, William, Stephen and I – that's why we're here."

"Aye" came from Stephen.

"Never heard of Dundaff," said Fraser, "But anywhere that's quiet seems a guid idea the noo. Ah guess we'll no' be welcomed guests in mony toons whaur there's English. Ah'll be alangside ye."

John put the goblet from his mouth. "Weel, ah suppose ah'd better come alang tae. Ah believe there might jist ha'e been some deeds done alang the way that might need some confessin'. Be bad if ye had tae look fur another priest tae dae that confessin' tae. Ken whit ah mean. He might no'be jist as understandin'."

I thought back to my last confession at Cuilross and the kindness of Father Ambrose. It wasn't a daydream, just a quick second of reminiscence, but, coming out of it, all eyes were on me. Presumably to also make my affirmation of support.

"I'm leaving," I said.

CHAPTER THIRTY THREE

The Road Back to Faukirk

"And ah was thinkin' it was aboot time fur ye tae gie us a sang, ma singer." It was Wallace. "Nae sangs, then?"

"I just thought that this would be a good time to..". It was more of a stutter than an answer.

"Time tae what?"

"No time's a guid time," said Fraser. From his reply, I could guess where his sympathies lay but I didn't think he added much to the discourse.

"I don't know. It's just I can't be so close without trying again. This time I feel I'll find her."

"Pish," commented John, adding even less to the discourse.

"It'll only be while you're all resting up. Once I've found her, I'll come back and join you."

"Aye, you do that, singer, you do that. Noo, gi'e us that sang," said Wallace.

My mouth was dry, but the opportunity to move on from the conversation was too good to ignore. I gave them a song. It wasn't my best and it didn't seem to be appreciated, but it brought the evening to a close.

I left in the morning, walking. They needed my mount as well as what his uncle could supply. But it wasn't far. I left without much fanfare, without much warmth and with a disbelief in the air that I would join them again. I started walking with a heavy heart. But as my footsteps lead me closer to Faukirk, a spring reappeared in them. Of course I was doing the right thing. I couldn't be this close to Meg and not look for her. I remembered my previous prayer, 'Help me find Meg again'. I prayed again.

I had been following the course of the River Carron. My friends would do likewise but follow it inland till they reached the ford. I was following it as it made its way to the River Forth. I came across what looked like an old Roman road which should take me to

Faukirk, so I started taking that. It led me through a very heavily wooded area and then to alongside a river. My guess was that it was still the same River Carron which had taken a meandering route while I had taken the straight one. On a whim I started to follow the river again.

It was a fairly easy walk as the tree line did not come right down to the river bank. There was plenty of wildlife and birds and birdsong to keep me occupied and it wasn't long before I was competing with the birds in a song competition. The thing was, there wasn't any people. Without people, there wasn't any chance of food. It wasn't immediate but it would soon become a priority. Perhaps I would have been better taking the straighter road.

Then, in the distance, I saw what looked to be huts. If they were inhabited, while they might not be a source of food, they would surely be a source of water. My footsteps quickened. As I got closer, I could see how unkempt the huts were. Wooden, but wooden with pieces missing. Shelter, but not from storm or heavy rain. If anyone lived there, it was a difficult existence.

Then a woman came out. It looked as if she was gathering water from a barrel at the side of the hut. I didn't want to frighten her by shouting, so instead I began running to catch her before she went back into the hut. She obviously heard the sounds of my feet and stopped and turned. She was quite young and very beauti.......

Meg.

CHAPTER THIRTY FOUR

Catching Up

If St Paul saw a vision on his road to Damascus, it was no greater vision than I had then.

"Alan," she cried, and ran towards me. We fell, almost literally, into each other's arms. And we hugged and hugged. And with each hug, our bodies seemed to want to get even closer. Not even to let the little breeze there was come between us. Neither of us said much. The best each of us could manage was to repeat each other's names. When we broke apart, there were tears running down both our faces.

She was still as beautiful. Still the same blue eyes. Still the same fair hair. Still with these red cheeks like apples. She was beautiful. She was Meg.

"How are you here?" she asked. "How did you find me? Where have you been for such a long time?"

Then, without allowing me to answer, she kissed me. No two pairs of lips were more made for this. This was part of the memory I had carried with me though all my travels. I was about to attempt to answer her string of questions, but she started crying, and all I could do was hold her close again. As her head buried itself into my chest, I remembered again how small she was.

The best I could manage now was the sound of "Ssshh."

"I'm sorry," she said. "I didn't think I'd ever see you again. Since that time in Cuilross……..oh, how often I wished I'd never said 'duty first'."

"Meg." Although she had given me little chance, I realised that all I had said to her so far was repeating her name. This was not the time for my laconic conversation to return.

"Well, it was duty first, but here I am."

"How did you find me?"

"Well, you weren't at the kirk."

"That was really just a landmark. How could I describe this place?" She was right. We were several miles from Faukirk, surrounded by a forest, on the banks of a river and with no signs of any other human habitation. "So how did you find me?"

"It's a long story," I replied.

"I seem to remember I liked your long stories."

I had thought of this moment often. Would she be the same? Would it be awkward? What would I say to her? Would she now be with someone else? And yet, here I was and she made it as easy as it was the first time she emerged from behind the rock. And surely she wouldn't have rushed into my arms like that if there had been someone else.

"Do you know it was maybe luck or maybe God? I was coming to find you. But I was going back to look in Faukirk. Then something told me to take the path that led here."

"Back?"

"Aye. I was there before, but nobody could help me. No-one knew of this seller of nails, or her father."

The tears can back to her eyes and her gaze left mine to look across the river.

"He died."

"I'm sorry."

"He was an old man. But my life was to look after him. He couldn't do a lot for himself. I miss him. I thought I should move from here when he went, but there's still too much of him around." Her eyes came round from the river and settled on the hut. "We didn't have much, but we survived on what I made."

"I'm sure he was more than grateful to be looked after by his daughter."

I got the feeling that something was changing. From her being glad to see me to not being glad to see me here, perhaps.

"Would you like a drink? I don't have anything other than rain water."

"I couldn't imagine anything better." She started to walk towards the hut. I stretched out my hand and took hers. And that smile broke out all over her face again. It was as if the smile on her lips told her red cheeks to carry the joy to her eyes. In that second, my Meg was back. This time I kissed her.

She poured me that drink and we sat outside the hut while I told her a little of my story. Perhaps I told her a little bit more of my time in France than I did of my subsequent time in Scotland, but then she didn't know me as a fighting man. I did tell her of Wallace, but she hadn't heard of him.

It wasn't surprising really as she recounted her story. Yes, she still traded salt for nails and so still did the ferry crossing to Cuilross, but she sold the salt to a merchant for the provisions she needed, mostly oats or meal, so she was seldom actually in Faukirk. Therefore she heard little news.

The conversation flowed so easily, first one way then the other, as we filled in the gaps of which each other had been doing. Then it seemed to come to slow down suddenly if not come to an abrupt halt, and the smiles disappeared.

"So, Alan, what about these French women?"

"Oh, they were nice," I replied, feigning as much innocence as I could.

"Nice?"

"Yes, most that I met. Mind you, you don't meet too many in the sanctuary of Notre Dame."

"And was there one special one?"

I took her in my arms again. "Meg, there wasn't a special one. There wasn't anyone. I haven't been with a woman since being with you." Although it was true, somehow it didn't sound as true and sincere as it should. "Believe me?"

"I think I do."

"And you? Any men in your life?"

"What here? No men come here. Or at least the ones who do are either too old to care or too old to defend themselves if they dare make a move towards me. No, Alan, no men have been in my life. Not since you."

She got up. "Do you want to come inside, my lay brother?" And her smile returned.

"I would love to," I replied. And she led me into her hut. And she took me to her bed. And we lay down. And we made love.

CHAPTER THIRTY FIVE

At Camelon

And we made love and we made love and we made love.

It was a wonderful time. Sometimes we made love because we wanted to. Sometimes we made love because we couldn't help it. Sometimes we made love because there was so much time to be made up.

But life also went on. The hut Meg lived in was in a terrible state and I spent a lot of time making it watertight. Then there were the pieces of furniture which needed strengthening. The baskets which she used for fishing also needed repair. And so on. It was a good life, but it was a domestic life.

I stayed more or less around the hut and we only took the occasional foray into Faukirk to take Mass and the equally occasional Confession.

Meg still carried on her trading. Still going across to Cuilross. I didn't ever go with her. It seemed that there was my past life. Here was my present life.

That present life made weeks become months. The days passed quickly with the work. The weir in the river she used to catch fish had to be fixed. But there were plenty of oysters and mussels and cockles when the fishing wasn't good. I started trapping in the forest like her father had done. And we still had the merchants coming to trade, bringing her nails and the food we couldn't grow or catch, though Meg's need for defence had disappeared.

We spent Christmas of the year 1296 in that hut. I was happy. We were happy.

But as the days went on, I couldn't help but wonder what had happened to John, to Fraser and to William. They couldn't still be resting. So what were they up to? Had they gathered men again? Had they started another journey of liberation? Or had they had enough? Was it someone else's turn now?

But I only needed to look at Meg as she came up from tending the fish traps, with the smile on her face, with her laugh always ready to come to the surface, to banish these thoughts. We heard little of what was going on in Scotland here and maybe it was better this way.

It must have been around the month of May, I was working clearing some ground when I heard a horse approaching. We had very few visitors and we weren't expecting any merchants. I looked up to see by the robes he was wearing that it was a priest who was riding towards our house. (I had spent a lot of time and effort on the place since I had arrived, so it had been elevated from a hut to a house.) I stopped digging and pulling, as much to give my back a rest as anything, and watched as he came closer. I couldn't believe it. It was John – John Blair.

It was with real joy we welcomed each other. There was much back slapping and noises of greeting. Then the inevitable, "How did you find me?", echoing Meg's question when I first arrived here.

"Och, it wisnae that difficult. Us priests have oor ways."

"What do you mean?"

"Weel, ah knew ye were somewhaur in Faukirk. So ah jist asked the priests there. Maybe ye should watch how much ye're confessin'."

"Oh, it's good to see you, John."

"Aye, an' you, Alan. So ye found yer Meg then?"

"I did. I was in luck. And I didn't have any priests to guide me. How about the others? Fraser, William? How are they doing? What are they doing? How have you been yourself?"

"Steady, mon, steady. Wull ye no' introduce me to this Meg, this wuman who has kept ye frae us?"

"She's not here right now. She'll be back this afternoon. Plenty of time for you to tell me what's been going on. You'll be wanting a drink first. I've plenty water in the barrel."

I had been apart from John too long. He got up, reached into his saddlebag and produced a flagon. Wine no doubt. "Ye'll jine me?"

"I will that. It's been a long time."

"Then get ye some beakers an' gie ma horse some water, then we can talk."

I did as requested, though a request from John sounded more like a command. And we settled down on the river bank. He poured the wine, though I couldn't help but notice, disproportionately.

"So now. Fraser and William? How are they?"

"Oh, still fightin'."

"I wouldn't have expected less."

"Aye, an' winnin'. William says tae tell ye that there's little point in winnin' if there's no a sang at the end o' it."

"I'm sure he gives it little thought."

"Oh, he gives it thought a' right. He wants ye tae come back an' jine him."

I took a large draught of the wine. "Right."

"That's why ah'm here. Dae ye think ah came a' this way jist tae see how ye were getting' oan?"

"Well, you can see I'm getting on fine. Meg and me are doing fine."

"Ah'm sure ye are. But she'll aye be here when ye get back."

"I'm not sure I'm leaving, John."

"And whit'll ye be stayin' for. Tae mind this wee bit o'land? When they fin' oot ye've goat it, they English'll tax ye tae pay fur Edward's war in France. Come back wi' us. Make yer land Scots again. Do weel an' ye might get mair land yersel'."

I tried another draught of the wine, but my beaker was already empty. "And Meg"

"Man, she managed afore. She kin manage again."

"Maybe."

"Maybe? Look, man, it's stertit."

"What's started?"

This time it was John who paused while finishing his wine. Then he turned and looked at me. "Independence, Alan, independence."

CHAPTER THIRTY SIX

Another Reunion

I had never known an afternoon pass so quickly. John didn't return to the question of me leaving with him, but rather started telling me of the events that had happened while I was here with Meg. The stories were almost incredible.

We knew Edward had marched into Scotland last year. I remembered how I felt when I learned Balliol had surrendered to him at Brechin. But I didn't know the full details of the bloodbath at Berwick or the submission of the Scottish nobles and knights at the so-called Battle of Dunbar. Every one of John's tales made me feel more and more Scottish. Made me wonder what right the English had to do this to us.

We moved inside and poured more wine. John waited a bit. I suppose he waited keeping the most important story till last.

He almost took a deep breath, then started. Wallace had been in Lanark. He had been dragged to court by William Hesilrig, the Sheriff of Lanark. Some trumped up charge that he had not signed a Roll, showing his allegiance to Edward. Wallace vigorously defended the charge, arguing that his elder brother, Malcolm, should have been the one to sign. According to John, he was with Richard de Lundie at the time and, as the argument heated up, Wallace eventually declared that he would never give allegiance to Edward. As this was treasonable, Hesilrig attempted to have him arrested. In the fight that followed, Lundie and Wallace killed the Sheriff, before escaping from Lanark with their men.

"When was this?" I asked.

"On the Day o' the Finding o' the Holy Cross," replied John. He looked at me. "Are ye no' acquaint wi' the Church's calendar?"

"I can manage Christmas and Easter. Too many other days to remember."

"Aye, weel. Jist two weeks ago. The third o' May."

"And Wallace is all right?"

"Did ah no' jist tell ye he wants you tae jine him? Aye, he's fine. Mair men are jinin' him every day. The killing of Hesilrig has stertit somethin'. Time fur you tae jine tae."

Whatever my reply might have been, it was interrupted by the door opening and Meg standing there.

"Ah saw the horse. Ah guessed we have company," she said, looking at John a little warily.

"This is John – John Blair. I've told you about him," I said. John stood up and made to kiss Meg's hand. She deftly got rid of the bag of salt she was carrying. These hands of John's that I had seen wield a sword in earnest seemed to take on another form, as if an angel had touched them with gentleness, as he kissed her hand.

"Ah kin see why Alan wanted tae find ye," he said. "Ye're a fine lass."

"An' you're a man of the cloth," she replied. "Alan's told me about you. You're welcome here."

"Ah thank ye fur that."

"How did ye find us?"

"It wisnae that difficult."

"He just asked the priests at Faukirk and somehow they knew," I interjected. "The same priests who knew nothing when I was looking for you."

"Are ye staying?" Meg asked, almost as if this was a conversation between John and her and I shouldn't be interrupting.

"That might be imposin' on yer hospitality", John replied. Meg caught my eye. I couldn't decide if she was wanting my affirmation or if she was warning me not to make any signs of encouragement, but I gave her a slight nod anyway.

"We have food and I can do something about a bed. Might no' be comfortable but it'll have to do."

"Yer welcome is only exceeded by yer hospitality," John said by way of acceptance. That angel had also crept in to his vocabulary.

"Ah'll start getting a meal ready." And with that she went back outside. Although she was gone, there was no doubt that she had left a coolth in the temperature. It was John who broke the silence.

"Fine woman."

"Aye, she is that. It's good here."

"Meanin'?"

"Meaning I can't just leave her and march off."

"Aye, I can see that. Ye'd rather stye wi' her here an' wait till ye become English."

"How long will it be?"

"Afore ye're English?"

"No. How long will I need to be away?"

"The rate men are jinin' Wallace, no lang. There's risin's in the west coast as weel. Ha'e ye heard o' Andrew Moray?"

"No."

"He owns land up north. Edward's goat his faither in jail in London. He wis in jail himself, but goat oot. Anyway, he's come oot in defiance o' Edward and the men up north are jinin' him. Alan, it's startin'. Whit did ah say tae ye earlier? Independence."

"So how long?"

"Ah dinna ken. It a' depends oan how mony o' us there are. There's trouble in Bute. And as ah say, Moray has taken Urquhart Castle and set fire tae Edward's ships berthed at Aberdeen."

"No, John. It'll be too long. I'm not leavin' Meg for that long."

"Someone speaking o' me?" Meg had opened the door and had obviously heard her name.

"And no' better subject tae be speakin' of," said John. More angels.

She placed a pot of porridge on the table. She put a little of her salt on a wooden spoon and laid it also on the table. "Ye'll give thanks, John?" she asked.

Now I had been with John for many weeks and many meals. Never had I seen him 'give thanks' before he ate. Come to think of it, Meg and I never did either. As I eyed him, I'm sure he almost winked and, in a voice I'd never heard before, intoned:

"In nomine Patris, et Filii et Spiritus Sancti. Amen."

We crossed ourselves, salted our porridge and had our meal. Our very quiet meal.

CHAPTER THIRTY SEVEN

My Meg

John did not stay the night. He left after the meal. For all his protestations of our hospitality, perhaps he thought meal time had been less than convivial. Perhaps he thought his journey had, to some extent, been fruitless. Whatever drove him, he rode off on his not fully rested horse. In the light of a Scottish summer evening, Meg and I sat outside. Meg took my hand.

"Go," she said.

"Go?"

"Wasn't that what John was here for? To get ye to go back with him?"

"Aye."

"Well?"

"Well what?"

"Well, why are ye still here?"

"I didn't want to go."

"Because of me?"

"Aye." She squeezed my hand and then kissed me, slowly, exploring all my mouth. "I love you, Meg."

"And I love you. But my love won't shackle you to this place. If go ye must, then must ye go."

"No. My place is here with you."

"And your duty?"

"Oh, if it were duty calling, I'd be back at Brechin. They might be wondering a little why they have heard nothing of their singing lay brother. Meg, I'm here with you. We don't need John or Brechin or anything else."

She smiled. And her smile broke into a laugh. "Then, Alan," she managed between the laughs, "It is I who demands you do your duty. Your duty to me as a man. If your John isn't staying, your other john can be useful." And she stopped laughing. "Bury yourself in me,

Alan. Not fondly, not gently. Make our bodies one for as long as possible. I want to feel you inside me."

She got up and offered her hand to me. "Come, my lay brother. Come." She was laughing again.

'Sorry, John, Scotland's independence will have to wait,' I thought.

CHAPTER THIRTY EIGHT

John's Story

Scotland's independence didn't have to wait too long.

It was on the 25th June, 1297 that John Blair rode back into our lives. Seeing him ride in, I recognised him immediately and ran to greet him. One look at his face and I could tell he was bringing with him news that he didn't want to tell and I didn't want to hear. Our greetings were muted.

Meg came out. She waved to John, but immediately sensed the atmosphere. She went to get drinks.

John settled down and, without invitation, began to tell us what had happened. Meg brought us drinks.

As well as bringing us news, he was also relating events in which he had taken part. As he spoke about them, you could see in his eyes that he was reliving them. He paused a lot. His silences spoke volumes. He had many silences as he thought again about what had happened. It was almost as if he couldn't believe what had happened, but he had seen it all with his own eyes. It had happened. The gist of what he told us was this.

Edward had got fed up with his 'Warden of the kingdom and lands of Scotland' John de Warenne for not returning to Scotland and taking charge and dealing with the rebels.

I started to interrupt John at this point, but he waved his hand almost in annoyance. I didn't try to interrupt again.

So Edward sent other knights to bring the populace to order. He also sent judiciary and one – Arnulf of Southampton – in particular. Arnulf decided to make a show in Ayr and, backed by plenty of English troops, set up an eyre-court.

While not interrupting, John must have seen quizzical look on Meg's face and explained that an eyre-court is just an itinerant court. Usually set up in places without court buildings and where the judge might come round once a year.

He set it up in a large building just outside of Ayr. The locals called it The Barns. He summoned all the leading Scots to attend. And a lot did.

The Barns had only one entry and Arnulf had it suitably guarded by English troops. Only one Scot was allowed to enter at a time. Once in, they were gagged and tied by more English soldiers. A noose was placed around their necks and they were hanged from the rafters. On that day three hundred and sixty Scotsmen were hanged. A court! Edward's justice.

A silent tear ran down Meg's cheek.

When Wallace heard, he was incensed. Two days later, at night, he led his men on a revenge attack. His main party he split into two. He had heard that Arnulf was still at The Barns and, with his men, had been carousing all night. He would lead his party there. He sent Robert Boyd with fifty men to Ayr Castle where the English garrison were quartered. And he sent John to the Priory with another eight men, as more English troops had been quartered there.

When he arrived at The Barns, Wallace waited until he established that his information was correct. The English had been drinking and were now sleeping off the effects. He surrounded the building with brushwood. On the brushwood he poured oil. He barricaded the only door – that door that the Scots had been allowed through one at a time to reach their untimely fate. Then he torched the place.

As the building lit up the night sky, the troops at Ayr Castle were wakened and rushed to aid their colleagues. But Boyd's party were waiting for them and they were all slaughtered.

John had informed the Prior of what was going to happen. When they saw the light from the burning building, they carried out their own revenge. One hundred and forty more English troops lost their lives.

By dawn, almost five thousand English troops had been killed.

His last silence was the longest. Then, "They shouldna ha'e done it."

"Oh, yes they should." It was Meg.

Her voice, or her words, seemed to awaken John from his reverie. "Ah meant the English. They shouldna ha'e hung oor men. They tak' oor country, then they kill oor folk. They tak' oor earth, then they kill the plants that grow in it. They canna dae it. It's oor land." And this time a silent tear ran down John's cheek.

Meg looked up at me. "Go," she said.

I moved to the kist and found my sword. Buckling it on, I realised it had been months since I had used it. But Meg's earlier words came to my mind: if go ye must, then must ye go. This time I had to go.

I looked to John. "Maybe you could get your horse ready to take the two of us?" I asked.

"Aye," he said and went outside.

"I'll be back," I said to Meg.

"Ah know ye will," she answered.

"I will. This is it. I must help." She came into my arms and held onto me as if wanting to remember what my body felt like. I could feel my heart beating against her breast. I gently moved her head up with my hands and we kissed. "I love you."

"Ah know ye do, Alan. And ah love you. Come back to me. And come back in one piece. We've still to have that son for you." We kissed again.

From outside, the sound of the horse told us it was time. I held her face in my hands and stared into those eyes – those eyes that I might not see again. It was Meg who broke the stare.

"Why are you still here?"

CHAPTER THIRTY NINE

Heading On

"Where are we heading?" I asked John as we rode out.

"We'll head fur Cambuskenneth. We'll fin' oot there where Wallace is and make tracks tae jine him."

Would that it had been so easy. Word reached us that Wallace was assembling his troops in Selkirk Forest. It seemed that more men were joining him all the time. He was going to train them while in the forest and make an army out of the miscellaneous groups and motley individuals who had joined his cause.

Good. We would head for Selkirk.

Then news reached us from Irvine. A force of English, the news said some three hundred cavalry and forty thousand foot soldiers, though John thought this must be an exaggeration, had crossed the border and headed for Ayrshire. The Scottish nobles and their men were encamped there. Was there a battle? Not a bit of it. The nobles were still arguing about who should lead them and, not finding resolution to this difficulty, decided after two days to surrender to the English. My grip on John's concept of 'independence' was becoming looser. But John's summation was more pithy and more John-like.

"Pish."

Wallace had not been at Irvine. If he had, perhaps the outcome would have been different. We would head for Selkirk.

Then more news arrived that Wallace had attacked the English baggage train as it retreated in triumph. Word was that some five hundred English soldiers were killed and that Wallace was awash with booty from the escapade. We would head for Selkirk.

The next thing we heard was that Wallace had taken Glasgow by storm. Three hundred horsemen storming across Glasgow Bridge. What a sight. But seemingly Antony Bek, who controlled the area for Edward and who was Wallace's target, escaped.

This brought another expletive from John. “Yon’s no’ a proper priest that Bek. Oh, he might ha’e been oan crusade wi’ Edward, but that doesnae stop him bein’ a bastard.”

As the epithet was one that John conferred on most English, I didn’t show over excitement. Then John added:

“He’s the same wee bastard that took the surrender of King John to Edward at Brechin. Remember?”

Now I remembered. “Pish,” I said. We would head for…..Glasgow.

But every time we prepared to leave and catch up with Wallace, further news reached us. He had headed for Dunduff. We would head for Dunduff. He had stationed most of his men at Strathtfillan. We would head for Strathfillan. He had met up with more resistance troops at Glendochart. We would head for Glendochart.

While it was gratifying to hear of Wallace’s exploits and to realise that he was building an army, it was frustrating to be holed up in Cambuskenneth not making any useful contribution. John’s frustration was worse than mine and his demeanour, never tranquil at the best of times, resulted in several squabbles with the resident monks. Indeed the Abbot, Patrick, eventually required us to leave. Where we headed for, he didn’t care.

Then the unexpected happened. Wallace had sent a messenger to John telling him he was convening a Council of the nobles at Ardchattan. It was important for John to be there. We would head for Ardchattan.

John thought he would enjoy the process of telling Patrick that, yes, time we were really leaving.

“And where, may I ask, are ye heading for?” the Abbot asked.

“Ardchattan,” John replied, with one of his smiles reserved for his version of spreading peace.

“Ardchattan,” Patrick repeated. “Now there’s an interesting Priory there. Founded by Valliscaulians. Interesting order. They come from France. They decree that there must be no more than twenty monks in each monastery. And only the Prior is allowed any contact with the outside world.”

John tugged my arm to indicate we should leave as Patrick continued.

"The Valliscaulians have three Priories in Scotland. One at Pluscardon, one at Beauly and, of course, one at Ardchattan."

Another tug. I was in the process of creeping out with John when:

"When they started in France, there main income to support the order was the making of salt."

I was just becoming interested when John, rather than tugging, grabbed my arm and propelled me towards the door, still retaining his beatific smile, while Patrick continued seemingly unaware of our imminent exit.

"Of course, they didn't bring that skill to Scotland. No. I believe they grow kale….."

We were in the open air, and John obviously thought he could relax his facial muscles. "They made salt," I said, repeating our recently acquired knowledge, without in any way adding to it.

"So?"

"So that's what the monks do at Cuilross. I wonder if there's any connection?"

"Let's head there an' find oot."

"Head where?"

My head still hurts with the memory of the less-than-playful clout John gave me as his first response to my question. His second response was less sore, if also less precise:

"Ard-bastardin'-chattan!"

CHAPTER FORTY

Ardchattan

John's rush to leave the informed lecture that Patrick had begun had one flaw. We had no idea where Ard-bastardin'-chattan was and hadn't stopped long enough to ask directions. If Patrick knew so much about this obscure order, then he must have known how to get to them.

In a way I was sorry to be leaving Cambuskenneth. The monks there were very supportive of Wallace and we in turn benefitted from that support. I was sorry too about not finding out more about this salt thing. But neither factor seemed to influence John. His immediate priority was avoiding Stirling, reckoning he would get directions from somebody to somewhere after that.

We were sitting eating some bread by the roadside, watching our horses doing the same with grass, when he interrupted our individual thoughts with:

"Hiv ye ever heard o' Matthew Paris?"

"No," I replied.

"Benedictine. English. No' bad wi' the pen. Aye. Writer, historian, maker of Maps."

"So?"

"A first heard o' him when ah wis in Paris. He spent some time there. He's deid noo."

"So?"

"The man made a map o' the whole o' this island – north and south. Remember those maps ye were given when ye left Brechin?"

"They were hardly maps. More ways to get from one Abbey to another."

"Weel, they were mair detailed than Paris's map. Ye wouldnae get onywhere if ye were tae try followin' it."

"So what are you saying?"

"His map has a huge bit o' Scotland cried *Scocia Ultra Marina.*"

"Scotland under sea?"

"Scotland across the sea. But that's no' the point. Tae reach the north of Scotland by his map ye hiv tae go through Stirlin'. He's goat sea comin' in frae both sides leavin' it the only way tae get north. Noo we ken that's nonsense but ah think that is why the English still think Stirlin's so important. In their thinkin' it's still the only way north other than by sea."

I was letting this information permeate my brain, when John rose, threw away the rest of his bread, and mounted up. "Come oan. Let's find oot whaur we're goin'."

And that took us some time. Eventually we discovered that we should be heading for Loch Etive. This was some ninety miles of travel on some very rough roads and through some very rough terrain. But John was from far dismayed. "It's either that or we could head fur Selkirk," he said, with that smile lighting up his face.

Four days it took us. We even had to negotiate at one point to change horses. We came off worse on the deal. But arrive we did at Ard-bas……, at Ardchattan.

If the journey had been difficult, then it was almost forgotten by the welcome. Wallace had obviously watchkeepers stationed on the road leading in to the Priory. As a result, our arrival had been anticipated and there Wallace, that colossus of a man, stood waiting to greet us. John dismounted while his steed was still at the trot and ran into his arms. It was like brothers greeting each other after years apart. I dismounted and waited. Then:

"My Singer. Come." If my welcome was less physical than John's, it felt no less sincere. "Let us eat an' drink. Ye can tell me yer news an' ah can tell ye mine." And off he strode towards the Priory, still engulfing John in his arms.

Then, as if from nowhere, a familiar shape appeared. Fraser Campbell. His emotions soared as our handshake developed into a hug.

"Man," he said.

"Man," I replied.

"Better catch up wi' them, eh?"

"Yes," was the best I could manage.

As we followed, it was difficult not to see what was all around me. This was an army. How many men? A thousand? Two thousand? Things had changed since I was last with Wallace. He was in charge of all this? Maybe John was right after all. Maybe there was a chance to beat the invading army. Maybe there was a chance of this independence.

Such high thoughts were soon brought down to earth. When we sat in the refectory, we were served a potage of kale. Wallace saw my reluctance at finishing the victuals. He leaned over to tell me that this order of monks had been formed in Burgundy in the Val des Choux. My French quickly translated this as The Valley of the Cabbages. I guess the kale was as close as they could get.

"And salt?" I asked.

He looked at me quizzically. "Never mind," I said.

"We wouldnae be wantin' tae cause ony offence tae oor hosts," he added and gave me a wink. I lifted the bowl and finished it as if it were ambrosia.

There wasn't much news to be imparted on my side and Wallace seemed to want to distil his news. The Council had ended just before we arrived. Wallace had given back some lands taken off the English to some Scottish nobles. Before the Council he had been making waves over quite a lot of the land of Scotland. He talked of a battle at Glendochart. It seemingly could have gone either way, but eventually, after a couple of hours, he and his troops were victorious. But that was all he would say.

"Will ye gi'e us a song. Alan?" he asked. I wasn't sure if it was a genuine request or if it was a means of changing the subject.

"To celebrate another victory?" I asked, thinking of Glendochart. I was making up songs all the time. I didn't write them down, but by repeating them to myself I was able to learn my words and retain my tune. I had a song for him.

"No. No' this time. Jist tae cheer us a' up. Ah want tae talk tae everybody first, then ye can sing. An' be sure tae make it cheery."

He rose and banged his mug on the table. The room became quiet.

"Men, oor work is done here, oor time here is o'er. We must march on again. Ah ken ye ha'e wives an' families tae return tae. Ah ken ye're a' tired o' fightin'. But the time tae return is when every step you take oan that journey is on Scottish soil owned by Scottish people. Then we can a' stoap fightin'."

The room reverberated with feet, stamping out their agreement.

"So we will march. We will march on. Tell yer men that we leave tomorrow. We make fur St. John's Town."

This time there was a murmur in the room. Of course they knew the town was held by the English. But why St John's Town? It was on the other side of Scotland. A march of some ninety miles over some of Scotland's hills and mountains. But, whatever Wallace's reasons were, he was not prepared to share them at this time.

"We will make St John's Town Scottish again. We will clear the usurpers oot. We will chase them south and further south, until Scots land is oor land. An' Scots justice, oor justice. An' Scots priests, oor priests. So we will march. And every step will be a step fur oor land and oor King."

They were standing up - cheering. And I was with them. This is why I was here. This is why I left Meg. This is the journey we must make.

His long arms outstretched, he quietened the assembly. "Alan, a song," he commanded. The others sat back down. I felt their eyes on me. I had sung to Wallace many times before. I had sung in the great Cathedral in Paris in the choir. But this was the first time I had sung to so many by myself. Perhaps my voice was a little unsure to begin with, but it grew in strength. Perhaps it was the words.

My song is one for all to sing,
For all men join this lay.
We sing a song for Scotland's King,
To be crowned this very day.

Tho' Edward's troops oppression bring,
They will be made to pay.
We sing a song for Scotland's King,
To be crowned this very day.

Scotland's Freedom Bell will ring,
So ring it while ye may.
We sing a song for Scotland's King,
To be crowned this very day.

And they did join in! And by the end they were all standing again. And when we finished, they cheered. As loud a cheer as they gave Wallace. And William Wallace gave me another wink.

CHAPTER FORTY ONE

Liberating St John's Town

We rode out the next morning. Wallace led with John at his side. And on the other side? Me. Fraser was just behind. If I was proud last night with the singing, I was even prouder with the riding. Nothing could be better. Well, perhaps one thing. Wallace was humming my tune!

Although Wallace's objective was St John's Town, he led us on an even longer march, along the north shore of Loch Tay, until we reached Dunkeld. Here he established camp.

To me it seemed odd for Wallace to make Dunkeld his base. John Blair reckoned that it was because the Bishop, Matthew de Crambeth, was sympathetic to the Wallace cause. In fact, King John Balliol had sent the Bishop to France to negotiate on behalf of Scotland just a couple of years before. He was probably in Paris at the same time I was.

One of the nobles who had been at the Council at Ardchattan was Sir John Ramsay. He also marched with us to Dunkeld. Wallace sent him to St John's Town on a spying mission with Fraser. They had to report back on its defences. Their report was interesting. But one particular fact interested Wallace. It was Sir John's assessment that the town walls were quite low. He said they gave an impression of greater height as a moat had been dug in front of them. Wallace asked him to repeat this and followed up with some questioning. Then we were all dismissed.

The following day, Wallace called us all back together. He had a plan. He would build structures that would allow us to climb over the town walls. It took us all a little time to grasp what he was proposing.

His idea was to build ladders on platforms with a protecting roof to shield against arrows or rocks that might be thrown by the defenders. He would fill in parts of the moat with earth and stones, wheel the ladder structures in and breach the town walls. If there wasn't an overt display of enthusiasm, equally no-one demurred. Then it was Fraser:

"Aye, an' how dae we get them there?"

"We'll build rafts and float them down the River Tay," he replied.

And so it was decided. Wallace had the ability to inspire confidence even when battle hardy men would have been more likely to show scepticism. Local tradesmen were recruited and the building of the structure begun. Sir John Ramsay was again sent to St John's Town to estimate the proper height for the structures. The rest of us were engaged in preparing for battle, sharpening arms, fixing shields and catching up with some sleep. It took four days to complete the build. Then again confidence was tested as the rafts were launched into the river, as the ropes that pulled them were manipulated from the shore and as the process of getting them back onto dry land was completed. But in the end they were ready to move into position.

The next stage was not pretty. As the men filled in the moat at the points where the ladder structures would be pulled into place, so the English defenders cascaded large rocks on them. They had weapons which looked like oversized crossbows and they fired the rocks from them. At close range their archers didn't need to be precise in their aim as they rained their arrows down. Our troops had the difficulty of trying to protect themselves overhead with their shields while getting the earth and stones into place. But eventually they succeeded, with fewer casualties than might have been expected, and the ladder structures were moved into place.

John and I had been standing with Wallace as these preparations were going on. He now turned to us:

"Now, fightin' priest and fightin' singer, draw your swords. Today St John's Town will be ours." He called Sir John Ramsay and Sir John Graham over. "When we get ower the walls, you two tak' yer men tae the bridge. Ah'll head fur the centre. Dinnae touch ony o' the citizens, but tak' nae English prisoners." Then to the men he shouted:

"Today this town will be ours. This St John's Town. Jesus called St John a Son of Thunder. Now is your time to be Sons of Thunder. Mount the walls. Take to the streets. Slay the invaders. Men, our time is now. Forward."

And the charge began. With Wallace leading from the front.

The design of the ladders could have been better. We had the difficult bit of getting from the ladder to the wall with the protecting overhead shield in our way. But we managed it. And more and more of us managed it. It wasn't long before the defending troops nearest the wall were fleeing.

As I jumped down, a swinging sword caught me on the left arm and drew blood. My own sword returned the favour catching the recipient on the neck, and drew a lot of blood. As we pressed on, I could feel the blood pumping through my veins. Although most of the enemy were retreating, some stood their ground and had to be dealt with. My left arm might be damaged but my right arm was strong. The more my blood ran down my arm, the more English blood I wanted to spill.

After a couple of hours, we had all converged to St John's Church in the centre of the town. The town had been cleared. Well, not exactly cleared as there were bodies lying everywhere on the streets. It was an odd time for such a thought to come into my head, but I thought of the streets of Paris and the paving. Here the blood was making mud.

Wallace had fought his way through, remaining at the front at all times. As I caught up with him, we both just smiled at each other. He seemed to have little breath for speech. Then from nowhere he said:

"Scotland's Freedom Bell will ring." He must have seen my chest swell with pride. But, ever practical, he added, "Get that airm seen to."

He climbed onto some masonry and addressed the troops.

"Men, ye are Sons of Thunder. St John's Town is yours. But treat it wi' respect. Respect its buildings, respect its people. Respect also the bodies that lie here. Deal wi' them an' be thankful tae the Good Lord that it wasnae you. But, if the town is yours, then you must mak it yours. Tak' onythin' that belonged tae the English. It's yours. Tak' their food and tak' their drink. But didnae tak' their wimen. The town is yours, the night is yours."

As his men cheered, he climbed down. "Come oan, Alan. Let's find a place where we can put oor feet up. We deserve it. But there'll be no sangs the night."

He was right. Afterwards we found out that on that day there had been two thousand Englishmen slain.

CHAPTER FORTY TWO

Coming Back Home

Wallace found a comfortable abandoned house. We made ourselves at home. There was plenty of food and plenty of wine. We ate and drank and, from the noises coming from outside, we weren't alone in that.

There was quite a few of us. One of them was a knight called Ruthven. He had arrived with thirty men to join Wallace while the ladders were being built. Wallace had noted how keenly he and his men had fought that afternoon and had asked him to join us. I saw Wallace pulling him over to a corner and both of them engaging in what looked like a serious conversation. When Wallace re-joined us, he explained that he had asked him and his men to stay and defend the town. He had appointed him Captain and Sheriff of St John's Town.

I couldn't help thinking back to Gargowans. Then he had such a small band of men he couldn't occupy the Peel Tower. Now he was an occupying force. Now he was occupying one of the biggest towns in Scotland. But I also couldn't help thinking that leaving a force behind meant we were on the move again.

"So we're moving on?" I asked.

"Aye. Tomorrow," he replied. The sound of revelry from outside drifted in again and I wondered how many would be fit to move on.

"Where?"

"North."

"Where north?"

"Dunnottar Castle."

"That far? Why there?"

"'Cause I need to retrieve my magic shield."

"Your what?"

"Can ye no' speak withoot askin' questions?"

"Sorry. What magic shield?"

"There ye go again. Ach, it's an old wives tale about someone cried Fergus retrievin' his magic shield at Dunotter."

"Right. But why Dunotter?"

"Alan! Because Edward took it last year and ah intend tae take it back. Because there's too many English troops all round that place. Because it's going tae be difficult tae take. Enough reasons?"

"Aye."

"But we're no' goin' straight there. Tomorrow we go tae Brechin."

"Brechin?"

"Don't stert that again."

"But Brechin's my home."

"Ah ken. And ah ken it's time ye went back." Leaving that hanging in the air, he walked away.

I was caught between two emotions. Of course I was pleased to be going back. But I also felt guilt at not having gone back sooner. It was where I grew up and there were friends there. But there was also Friar William who had sent me to France to come back with the new music. I will want to tell them about Meg. But they will want to hear about Paris. It was time I went back there.

We left the next day. Wallace had divided the men up. As we were riding, we were in the first group. The journey wasn't fast as we had a marching contingent with us.

We skirted Dundee as it was held by English troops and moved through Glamis and Forfar. As we did so, first small crowds, then larger crowds appeared to greet us. Country people have their own way of spreading news fast. Then we were on the last stage to Brechin. As we reached the outskirts of the town, we could see more and more people out. They were cheering. They were cheering us. It was like a triumphal procession.

Wallace initially seemed bemused but then he began to acknowledge the crowds and returned their waves. By the time we reached the Abbey, he was being positively regal in his gestures. And here the crowd was at its biggest.

And there standing at the very front was Friar William.

I dismounted and approached him tentatively, but he clasped his arms around mine. I gave an involuntary wince. My wound from yesterday had not yet healed.

"You do not look pleased to see me, Alan," he said.

"Sorry, Sire. My arm hurts a little. I am very pleased to see you."

"After all this time," he interjected.

"After all this time," I repeated.

"You will have much to tell me?"

"Much, Sire,"

"Good. " And turning away from me, "Wallace, William Wallace I take it. We have heard much of you. You are welcome, sir. And you?"

"Blair. Father John Blair."

"You too are welcome, Father," he said, though his face could not have been more contorted if he had stood on shit. "You are all welcome. You will join me in some wine?" He indicated leading us inside.

"If ye could indicate where I should billet ma men, ah'll see them settled first."

Not to be outdone, John came in with, "And if you could show me the altar, ah would first like tae gi'e thanks fur blessin's received and fur reachin' Brechin." Perhaps I had missed this religious John but I couldn't miss his contorted face, which showed a refinement on Friar William's. He could have walked through pig shit.

"Of course," said William. "Alan, you make for my cell while I sort things out here. I'll be with you shortly."

Oh, no. My memories of his cell were not good. Cold, uncomfortable, no seating and with its air imbued with foreboding for the future. But I made my way. I felt like a condemned man.

When I reached it and tentatively opened the door, it was as if nothing had changed. Perhaps the foreboding air had taken on the more tangible form of the smell of tallow. Another Meg? And my Meg. How was she doing? I must get a message to her. She'll be wondering where I am. Or what I'm up to. Or, at least, was I still alive.

My thoughts of Meg were interrupted by Friar William opening his door. He stepped forward once again to clasp me by the arms, but thought better of it and changed the capacious greeting to that of the more temperate handshake.

"Well, Alan."

"Sire."

"We appreciated your messages. We perhaps thought they could have been more frequent. But welcome they were."

"Thank you."

"So, I could ask you to tell us all that you have learned in your lengthy stay in France and in your absence since arriving back on these shores."

"Enforced absence," I interjected.

"Of course. Your enforced absence. But it would surely take far too long."

"Indeed, Sire."

"So, I had an idea. Tomorrow I will release the brothers from work in the morning. You will meet with them after Vigils and rehearse them in the new music. Then they will be able to sing a new hymn as part of Eucharist. Good idea, eh?"

If memory served me right, that only gave me about two hours of rehearsal time. With a bunch of brothers who had no inkling of part singing and were, if I were being charitable, mixed in their musical ability.

"Excellent idea, Sire. Just one thing..."

"Good. That is decided. Let us join the others in a glass of wine. I would be loathe to imagine that brother of yours… What's his name?"

"John."

"Yes, John. We may have to drag him away from his devotions to have a glass of wine. After all, prayer is something to be taken in small doses by those who are not used to the medicine." This time no longer the twisted face of the shit-smeller, but a face with a smile. Almost beatific. "Tomorrow our rafters will ring with your music."

"Yes, Sire."

CHAPTER FORTY THREE

To Dunnottar Castle

Breakfast followed early morning prayers. It was eaten in the customary silence. As I ate my oat gruel, I noted that salt had not yet reached the outflung reaches of Brechin.

When we had finished, Wallace used the opportunity of breaking the silence to address the table.

"Friar, Brothers, ah canna pit intae words ma thanks for yer hospitality. Tae feed an army this size is no' easy. And ah'm aware that mony wouldnae dae it given the fact that there are English troops no' that far away. So ma thanks tae ye all. But we canna tarry. We ha'e some English that want tae sae goodbye to oor land."

There was laughter and much banging of mugs on the table.

"So wi' oor thanks come oor goodbyes. We hope tae visit ye again in a free Scotland."

More cheering and banging of mugs.

"It has been our service to welcome you and sustain you," replied Friar William. "We pray that God's hand will be in all that you do and that His presence will bless you at all times." As he crossed himself, he looked across at John Blair who followed suit, if a little belatedly.

"Thank you." said William. "Noo men, get the others ready for the road. We wull leave shortly." And he stood up and started to leave the room. Friar William put his hand on my arm to prevent me standing. I could almost swear he estimated the area of my wound as his placement was so accurate.

"But Alan will stay with us," he said. "He has work to do here."

John got in first with his answer, which was pithy if not prayerful.

"Pish."

Wallace immediately entered the vocal fray before Friar William had the chance to say anything.

"William." The use of Friar William's Christian name as the vocative without any appendage was evocative. Everyone looked at him as by one word he took command. "He comes with us. His work for us is now. His work for you can wait. Come, Alan."

Friar William's hand was withdrawn from my arm. I was released. More importantly, I was released from my two hours of choir duties, the results of which might not have justified my overlong stay away from Brechin.

We mounted our horses when everyone was ready and we set off. We set off north for Dunotter Castle.

And what a journey it was. Wallace led with some of us beside him. Behind us came the various banners with the St Andrew Cross at the front. Then came the cavalry, followed by the foot soldiers. This was a proper army.

If we thought the march into Brechin was special with the villagers along the way coming out to meet us, this was even more so. Everyone seemed to be out waiting for our arrival. Word of our coming preceded us. And the crowds. The children, the mothers, the farm labourers, the monks and priests – everyone. And they cheered as we rode past. Some picked flowers from the hedgerow and threw them to us. Others chanted Wallace's name. Some were crying. Others just beamed with pride. This was a Scottish army, marching on Scottish soil and they knew it and loved it.

Word of our coming had also reach Dunnottar Castle.

The castle sits on a promontory surrounded by the sea on three sides, which makes it fairly invincible. But once you scale its walls, there are few buildings inside. The main building is its wooden church, built of wattle and daub. I'm not sure what Wallace's plan was for conquering the place. It had to be from the front as without boats it was the only way of reaching it. And if we had boats, the castle sat high on cliffs which were almost impossible to scale. But no plan was necessary.

The news of our advancement had spread before us and all the English troops in the surrounding area headed for the Castle. Their fear overcame their ability to fight. We made one frontal attack and their defences crumbled. They nearly all crowded into the Church. So be it, thought Wallace. He barricaded them in and set fire to the church. A few put up some resistance but were soon put to the sword. Others looked at us and, rather than fight, jumped to their deaths off the cliffs.

The battle was easy, but I was left in two minds. On the one hand I remembered Friar William's blessing, that God's hand would be in all that we did. Well, He certainly made it easy for us. But was it God's hand that set alight His own house? Was it God's hand that sent so many inside to their deaths by flame? On the other hand, Wallace seemed unperturbed and gloried in his lack of casualties.

Again I didn't write a song for today's victory.

CHAPTER FORTY FOUR

Aberdeen Next

Wallace was fired up. His army was growing. His conquests were becoming easier. His land was being emptied of the English invaders. There was no question of stopping now. But where next? The answer was easy. The English based their headquarters for the region at Aberdeen. Aberdeen was just up the coast, a little to the north. So Aberdeen it was.

He told us the very night Dunottar Castle had been taken. We were having some food, kindly donated by the Castle's larder, when the conversation went something like this:

"Aye, weel, the troops'll be well fed the night," said Fraser. "We'll ha'e tae watch where we go next. There's a lot o' mouths ate feed."

"Could be a problem some time in the future. But no' the noo," replied Wallace. His assertion brought a quietness to the table. Fraser pressed on.

"Meanin'?"

"Meanin' we head fur Aberdeen."

"Pish." We all knew who made the interjection.

"So whit's wrang wi' Aberdeen, John," asked Wallace.

"Too mony bludy priests fur ma likin'," was his reply. "The reds and the blacks."

"That surely must mak it a holy place, John. An' ye like holy places." Wallace was teasing him.

"Wholly pish," was John's response.

"What do you mean 'the reds and the blacks'?" I asked.

"Och, ye get used tae the Black Friars, the Dominicans. But up there they ha'e Red Friars as weel, the Trinitarians. Ye kin get too much o' a guid thing."

"An' you could be handy fur a change, Alan," resumed Fraser. "Hauf o' them speak French up there wi' so mony frae Flanders."

"Ah don't intend tae dae much speakin'," was Wallace's retort.

We arrived at the outskirts of Aberdeen encountering no opposition. While there were fewer crowds to greet us, there were no signs of any English presence at all. Wallace sent Fraser Campbell with a small group into the town to scout and find out what was happening before he made entry with the whole army.

He returned with the news that the English troops were all loading up their ships in the harbour. He couldn't count them all but he estimated that there must be about one hundred ships. And, as far as he could see, they were all fully laden.

"So plenty for all these mouths, eh?" asked Wallace.

"Aye, looks like it," added Campbell as a rejoiner.

Wallace left us, his stride indicating he had business on his mind.

"It willnae just be food an' provisions. Looks like they're takin' a' their possessions wi them tae," continued Campbell.

"A just reward then fur these men if we can tak' the ships. A disappointment if they sail away," was John's contribution.

"Will he attack?" I asked.

"Will he no'," was John's reply. And so it was. Wallace had gone off to find out the times of the tide at the harbour. At low tide, the ships would be almost stranded, their keels stuck on the sea-bed. They would have to await the high tide to sail out. And the full low tide came at night.

Wallace positioned his troops and waited and watched the sea retreat. He had enlisted the services of a local fisherman so that he could judge the right time for the attack. It had to be when the ships were vulnerable and no longer floating, but also leaving enough time for Wallace's men to discharge the cargoes before being caught by the incoming tide.

The fisherman gave the signal to Wallace. Wallace gave the signal to his men. The battle began.

It wasn't much of a battle. Wallace had the numbers and they didn't take long to scale the ships. Once on board the fighting was hand to hand. This was their expertise. Swords slashed and stabbed. Bodies gasped and collapsed. It was soon over.

The Scottish army helped itself to its 'just reward' then set fire to all the English vessels. Wallace, still astride his horse, sat watching.

Word reached him that the English Sheriff of Aberdeen in charge of Aberdeen Castle, Sir Henry de Latham, no doubt seeing what was happening round about him, had defected to the Scots side. The last bastion in Aberdeen, the Castle, was now in Scots hands. A smile spread across Wallace's face.

But he still sat watching. He watched until that full tide came in, covering almost all of the burnt out ships in the harbour.

I ushered my horse forward to get beside Wallace and get his orders, but John, seeing my first movements, quickly turned his horse in front, stopping me advancing.

"Leave him," he said.

"I was only……".

"Leave him. He needs this time. And he needs it alone."

We backed our horses off until there was some distance between us and Wallace. Only then did John continue.

"That man is in charge o' most o' Scotland. Kin ye imagine whit it feels like. There's only Dundee an' Stirling left tae conquer. Then Scotland's his – or Balliol's."

"So what's next?"

"Ah dunno, Alan. Ah dunno."

There was a whinny from Wallace's horse. He had pulled it round. He rode up to join us. He pulled the horse up. He looked at us.

"Time ah met Andrew," he said.

CHAPTER FORTY FIVE

Towards Dundee

We had heard quite a lot of Andrew de Moray. In many ways he was doing what Wallace had been doing but in the very north of Scotland.

He had been imprisoned by Edward at Chester, but had managed to escape last year. After making his way back to his home turf, he started his own rebellion. He conquered many of the castles in the north which were held by the English, including Castle Urquhart which overlooked Loch Ness, and had control of much of the land.

Wallace had been told that a few weeks before he took Aberdeen, Edward had instructed a group of 'loyal' Scots to march on de Moray and restore Edward's royal authority in the region. Rather than retreat at the thought of this advancing force, de Moray had marshalled his men and marched to meet this English-supporting army. They met at Enzie, where the road from Aberdeen to Inverness forded the waters of the River Spey. The problem was that they were two Scots armies and neither had the stomach for the bloodshed of fellow countrymen that would ensue if they engaged in battle. They didn't. Both withdrew without a fight.

It was, perhaps, with this in mind that Wallace sent messengers to de Moray suggesting a meeting at Enzie. Time and place agreed, a small group of us rode out with Wallace.

As we arrived, de Moray was already there with a small retinue, all mounted. Wallace halted, but keeping some distance between them. It was de Moray who spoke first:

"Wallace?"

"Andrew," came Wallace's reply. We all noticed the use of titles. Here was the scion of one of the most important and influential families in Scotland, his father had been Justiciar of Scotia, the most senior legal office in Scotland (though currently serving Edward's pleasure in the Tower of London), addressing Wallace by his family name. Wallace, of low birth and no claim of right to be leading a rebel force, chose to reply using de Moray's Christian name.

"We should talk."

"Aye," came Wallace's succinct reply.

"Perhaps better off our horses?"

"Aye," came again the abrupt response. It didn't augur well for this 'talk'.

Wallace dismounted and threw his reins to me. He walked across to de Moray as he was dismounting. Then the two of them walked away from both sets of supporters. Then the talk quite clearly began. Then we saw de Moray put his arm around Wallace's shoulders. Then we heard laughter. Then we dismounted. This, then, was obviously going to take some time.

And take some time it did. But when they did eventually choose to return to the two sets of supporters, who had chosen to remain apart, it was evident that, in the developing flame of independence, a friendship had been forged. Wallace took the initiative.

"Andrew, you should meet some o' ma men."

"Likewise."

And so introductions were carried out. It was obvious to both sets that their leaders had made some kind of bond and so it behoved us also to start forging similar bonds of friendship. That done, Wallace addressed the whole assembly.

"Ye hive a' been fightin' fur Scotland. In different pairts, true. But wi' the same intent. Tae hiv Scotland ruled by her ain. Ye've done weel in the north. We've done no' bad in the south. Noo we think it's time we jined thegether tae finish the job. Are ye fur it?"

The cheer almost sounded lukewarm. I was unsure as to whether this was the result of a rousing speech being given to such a small audience, or whether it indicated a lack of enthusiasm for the suggestion. Wallace also hesitated. He was used to a more positive response. Hearing the pause, de Moray stepped in:

"This land, this Scotia, this Scotland is ours. Ours to rule with a just hand. Ours to rule with fairness. Ours to rule as brothers. We can all walk away now. But in time, when he's finished with the French, Edward will be back. What we have gained, he will take away. Where we have our own people in control, he will appoint his placemen. When that happens, all we have fought for will be lost.

Once again our Scotland will become his. No man living has done more in such a short time than William Wallace to take back our country. Now we should march together to take the rest. There's only two strong towns still in English hands – Stirling and Dundee. Now is the time to rid them of those English occupiers. We will march on Dundee. We will march with Wallace and myself at the front. Then we will take Dundee. We will make it ours." He too paused and looked around. "Are you for it?"

This time the cry did go up. The small audience found a big voice. The cheers echoed around the countryside. Then, from the back of de Moray's party, came the first quiet but insistent sounds of, "Dundee, Dundee." Almost as quickly those of us who had ridden in with Wallace picked up the rhythm and joined in. "Dundee, Dundee."

De Moray looked across at Wallace. Both smiled at each other, before joining in the chorus of "Dundee, Dundee."

Two men had come together. Two parties of supporters had come together. Soon, when each grouped joined the rest of their ranks, two armies would come together. A Scottish army to free Scotland.

So, Dundee it would be.

CHAPTER FORTY SIX

To Dundee

The march from Aberdeen to Dundee was only some seventy miles, but Wallace now realised that the planning and organisation of the movement of what was now a large force with their equipment and supplies had to be managed. After talking with de Moray, he made Fraser Campbell in charge of organising the troops and John Blair in charge of organising supplies.

We were still in Aberdeen waiting for the main part of De Moray's force to join us when all this was being decided. I happened to be with Blair when Wallace approached him.

"A' right?" was Wallace's introduction to the conversation.

"Aye. Wouldnae mind if there was a wee bit less rain fur this time in August. Bloody wet," was John's response. They could have been discussing farming in the valley of the Clyde rather than being in the middle of a campaign.

"As lang as yer thrapple gets wet," continued Wallace. "An' there's plenty o' wine aff them ships."

"True, true."

"Ah've bin thinkin' aboot how we'll tak it a' wi' us. An' the food as well."

"Ah'll manage enough in baskets wi' ma horse."

"Aye, but we canna ha'e men marchin' carryin' a' that fur themselves. Slow us doon. We need tae get organised wi' cairts an' stuff."

"Aye, ah suppose yer right."

"An' ah think yer jist the man tae dae it."

"Whit? Organise cairts?"

"No' jist. Ah'm gonna get Campbell tae divide up the men intae groups. What we need is tae work oot how much food an' drink each group will need an' organise enough cairts tae tak it wi' them."

"An' ye need a man o' the cloth tae dae that?"

"Ah need a man who's expert in drinkin' an' eating." And, with a laugh, Wallace walked off.

"Pish," was all that John could manage to offer to the departing back.

I wasn't there when Wallace met with Fraser Campbell to give his instructions about organising the troops. It wasn't until afterwards that Fraser recounted the gist of the conversation.

Wallace wanted the army broken into groups. As far as possible, he wanted his own men mixed with de Moray's men. The archers had to be kept separate as had the cavalry. He told Fraser not to include the ponies and nags but just the real war horses, somewhere just over a hundred.

"An' ah suppose ah'm expected tae find the feed for the horses as well," said John. The three of us were sitting together, John having brought with him a barrel of ale.

"Aye, jist," replied Fraser, a little unsympathetically. "An' ah've goat tae find a way of dividin' up some six thousand men. Ah'd rather be feedin' them than dividin' them tae tell ye the truth."

"Seems no' that difficult tae me. Six lots o' a thousand. Whit's yer problem?"

"A thousand's too big. Needs tae be smaller."

"Aye but ye stairt wi' the big. Someone commands a thousand, then ye break the thousand up."

The detail of this conversation went on for some time and, to be honest, I hardly participated. But the two of them got quite excited about it all, or the ale was having more and more effect. The bits of the argument that made most sense to me were that you wanted to keep men of the same clan together but you required small units if you wanted to be able to react quickly in a battle situation.

Eventually it was decided that the smallest unit would be of four, that unit could be could be doubled or trebled and the overarching biggest size would be a thousand. A lot of ale had been consumed before naming the groups. As usual, John held his ale best and seemed to make some sense, though Fraser nor I knew whether his knowledge of the scriptures was deeper than we thought or whether the ale was the mother of invention.

"Ye see, when St Peter was imprisoned he had four groups o' four Romans watching him in turn. They wis ca'ed a quatern. So oor wee groups could be quaterns. And when St Paul had his troubles wi' the Romans, the chief Roman was cried a Chiliarch, an' he wis in charge o' a thousand men," was John's insightful input.

It may have been just because it was late at night or maybe Fraser was actually convinced by John's arguments, but, whichever, the names stuck. I have no memory of where the name for the quaterns, when they were doubled or trebled, came from. The commander of them became known as a Decurion. My little Latin suggests that 'dec' should mean ten and my little adding up cannot get two or three fours to make ten, Maybe that was decided really late at night.

So the march to Dundee commenced. It wasn't nearly so orderly as Fraser wanted. Some men decided they didn't like the group they were assigned to and just changed. Not all commanders had been appointed so there was no real chain of command. But, all that being said, it still looked an impressive sight with the ranks of spearmen, their spears some twelve or fourteen foot high, marching alongside each other, followed by the ranks of archers and with the war horses taking up the rear.

John Blair, with a small party had ridden on ahead, to organise the provisions. It took me back to my first ride to Dundee, way before France, with John. I admired then his ability to go up to unknown houses and return with food and drink for us. His new role would really test that skill.

So, Dundee it was.

CHAPTER FORTY SEVEN

To Stirling

The taking of Dundee itself did not present any problems to our forces. The castle, however, was a different story. It was well-defended and, without building siege towers and other equipment, it was not going to be easy to breach. De Moray and Wallace decided that, as long as John could keep the army provisioned, a siege would eventually drive the defenders out without loss of life on our side.

In many respects, this delay proved to be advantageous. While Fraser had done his best to organise the troops, Wallace, and particularly de Moray, could see that there was still much to be done in making them a disciplined fighting force. So he used this time. He appointed new commanders and ordered new colours to be made so that every man knew who was his leader and could identify the colours he should follow.

He had the archers out practising. Most of the archers came from the Ettrick Forest and were highly skilled. The yew for their longbows came from Belgium, but their skill came from practising. De Moray was overheard to say how much he admired them, but that he could do with many more.

Wallace was restless at this time. I don't think Dundee was his favourite place. Maybe it was a hangover from his youth. We had all heard the story, though I never heard Wallace confirm it, that he was in Dundee completing his education as a youth. This day, he was playing with a ball on some land which had been designated for sport. A young Selby, son of the then Governor of Dundee Castle, approached him and told him that, as he was of low birth, he had no entitlement to wear a dagger in public. This insult so incensed Wallace that he drew his dagger to show Selby the skill he had with it. The result? One dead Selby and one outlawed Wallace. But I would have liked to have heard the story from Wallace's own lips.

But it was perhaps not just Wallace's past possible ploys that was making him restless. Word was constantly reaching us of the assemblage of the English Army.

John de Warenne, the Earl of Surrey – Wallace could hardly mention his name without spitting – had been appointed by Edward – and this was the bit that really annoyed Wallace – 'Warden of the Kingdom and land of Scotland.' Such was his love for the land of Scotland that he preferred staying back down in his own place in England. But now he had headed north. He had joined up with Cressingham's forces, said to be three hundred horse and ten thousand foot. Cressingham, the Treasurer of Scotland – the whole of Scotland could hardly mention his name without spitting – had been appointed by Edward to raise taxes in Scotland. He had ordered that all Scottish wool, Scotland's major export, be confiscated and sent to England. It wasn't because he was born illegitimate that he was called bastard up here. Instead of Treasurer, some even called him the Treacherer of Scotland.

Wallace told us that the English were marching through the Lammermuir Hills, through Lauderdale. There was only one place they could be heading…..Stirling.

John, Fraser and I were seeing a bit less of Wallace. He was spending more and more time with de Moray. From their time together, he would come back with a list of things needing done. More banners had to be made and had to be paraded to the troops so that they would recognise them and follow them in battle. More horns were needed and the specific sounds from them had to be taught and understood. Checks had to be made on which troops had the better armour. But the interesting one to Fraser and I were the exercises. Wallace had groups on men moving tightly together. They were usually six ranks deep and moved as one body. As all were armed with their long spears which rose above the group, they looked a formidable force to me and even to Fraser. There would seem to be no way horsemen could penetrate this enormous hedgehog. They began to be called Schiltrons, but, like the Decurions, I have no idea where the name came from. John Blair was less convinced by the sight, being more used to seeing hand to hand combat.

As we watched the drilling of the troops and the speed they could move and change formation, it was Fraser who summed it up effusively. "That's guid," he said.

John was no less effusive. "Pish."

All this while the siege was going on. But not for long.

Wallace and de Moray had decided they must reach Stirling before the English got there. Dundee Castle would have to wait. But not completely. He authorised a small group to maintain the siege and appointed one of his trusted commanders, Alexander Scrymgeour, to be in charge.

Perhaps realising that he had not spent as much time with us as normal, Wallace sought us out one night. As he came armed with some flagons of wine, it was obvious that the evening was for carousing, not caring.

After pleasantries, after drinking, after more drinking, the conversation became more natural, more like our conversations had been in the past. That gave Fraser the freedom to be more direct in his questioning.

"So, what's next?"

"Stirling," was Wallace's concise reply.

"When?" continued John.

"Two days."

I think there was a chorus between us. "Two days?"

"Aye. We need tae get there and choose our grun before the English arrive." There was a pause as we all thought about what he had said. Oh yes, we all knew it was coming, but now it was real. Two days.

"Will we win?" asked Fraser. It was the simple question we all wanted to ask, but didn't dare. We all knew that on this battle hung the fate of Scotland. It really didn't matter what we had won up till now. If we lost at Stirling, we lost everything.

"By God and Oor Lady's will, we will win," said Wallace. "An' choosin' the right grun."

If he meant it as a joke, none of us smiled. John Blair simply said, "Ah will pray fur that day."

"Oh, come on." It was Wallace again. "There's better company tae be had in a pile of shite. Gi'e us a sang, Alan. Cheer this place up. Naw, Ah'll stairt yer sang." And he did.

Scotland's Freedom Bell will ring,
And Fraser joined in. *So ring it while ye may,*
Then John. *We sing a song for Scotland's King,*
Then me. *To be crowned this very day.*
Yes, we will win.

CHAPTER FORTY EIGHT

The Abbot's Hill

If I thought the march to Dundee was impressive, then this march was really impressive. The ranks were in order and marched as their own unit. Each unit was marching behind its own new banner. Each commander rode in front of their own troops. I had never witnessed our army so organised. If Meg could only see this. And the pride emanating from them was almost tangible. A pride I shared as I rode as part of this Scotland's army.

The other good news about this march, compared to many others, was that the terrain between Dundee and Stirling was relatively flat. The troops didn't have any of the usual Scottish hills or mountains to encounter. That, and John Blair's astonishing ability to keep them supplied with food and drink, kept the morale very high.

Wallace and de Moray and a small party had ridden ahead leaving the main party under Fraser Campbell's overall control. Although Wallace knew the area around Stirling well, it was new to de Moray. And knowing an area well is different from knowing where to camp nearly seven thousand men and where to position them to give them the best advantage in battle. John Blair and I rode a little way behind the Wallace party, not being attached to any of the units in the main Army. Fraser Campbell was at the fore of the marching troops.

When we reached Stirling, Wallace stayed on the north side of the River Forth. The river itself had many loops and twists at this point, but, from that side of the river, Stirling Castle, which sits high on an outcrop of rock, could be clearly seen, about a mile and a half away. In front of Wallace stood the only bridge across the river. It was made of wood and built on eight stone piers. It wasn't very wide.

There was a causeway leading from it and it was on this track that Wallace and de Moray now stood.

"They've goat tae come over there," said Wallace, pointing at the bridge. "They're comin' frae the south an' they'll stop by the castle. Then here."

“Isn’t there a ford upstream or downstream?” asked de Moray, in an obvious attempt to verify Wallace’s statement.

“Aye, there’s wan, but it’s much further upstream. The wan downstream at Cambuskenneth depends on the tide.””

“Looks pretty boggy on either side of the track.”

“Aye, pretty swampy, but it’s fine here. Jist gets wet nearer the river. So, what d’ye think?” De Moray turned round on his saddle and looked behind him.

“That hill would give a good view of the surrounding terrain.” Behind them stood a large hill, an outcrop of rock which formed the end point of the Ochil Hills. As they looked at it, they could see the rock face, but they could also see that the hill was covered by a forest.

“Aye, it would that. An a’ this land and the hill is owned by the monks at Cambuskenneth Abbey. Good people. Nae fear o’ their allegiance.”

“Let’s get up the rock.” So they turned their horses round and negotiated a track which led them to the top of the hill. John and I were just onlookers at this point, but we followed on until they reached the top of the crag.

“Nice,” offered de Moray.

“Aye, gives ye a guid view o’ whit’s goin’ oan.”

“You can see the whole way to the castle.”

“Aye, an’ we’ll also see whit their troops are doing. Naewhere they kin hide.”

“We could run the battle from here, with our troops ready and concealed in the woods.”

“Aye, an’ we could mak’ camp jist behind the crag. That wye they canna see us.”

“And yet, within minutes, they can be down the hill. The big English warhorses won’t manage on that swamp so they’ll need to come over the bridge in pairs and stay in twos till they reach the better ground. Easy pickings for our spearmen.”

“Aye, I hope so. So that’s decided? We set up camp here?

“Yes,” replied de Moray, “We set up camp here.” Then Wallace shouted me over.

"Alan, ride back tae meet Fraser and get him tae bring the army here. John, get things set up doon there, but behin' the crag." And John was off...vocally.

"Doon there? D'ye ken how much room ah need tae set up camp fur a' these people? There's no enough room doon there. Ah'll need tae cut doon trees."

"Then, John, cut doon trees," came Wallace's reply.

"Pish." And off we went to do our various duties.

It was from that brief conversation and that quick decision that so much in the future depended. They had chosen this uphill site where both could survey the whole battlefield. Staying on this north side of the River Forth meant that, if the English troops had to engage with them, they had to cross a narrow bridge which would only allow them to move two abreast. When they reached the north side, the English warhorse could not spread out for an attack as, if they tried, their horses would become bogged down on the swampy ground. Nor could the English assess the size of the Scottish force as it could be hidden in the woods until summoned into the attack. It looked good.

The only question was whether Wallace and de Moray could get the troops all sorted out according to this plan before the English force actually arrived.

My only question was whether I could get Fraser to lead the whole Scots force to hide behind a hill and set up camp just because I told him to. I could only hope so.

There was no question. This was going to be our biggest battle.

CHAPTER FORTY NINE

Another Meeting

From the top of the Abbey Craig, thehill Wallace a de Moray identified, we watch the English setting up camp in the carse below.

Our camp was well established. Yes, and trees had been felled to create the necessary space. When our opponents had established theirs, battle would commence.

Wallace established a rota between us to keep watch on the developing camp. He had given us a horn – literally a sheep's horn – to sound if the developments required his attention. It was my turn on duty.

I could see two horsemen ride up to the bridge. They halted on the south side. Should I blow? They looked like knights. I couldn't see the emblems on their tabards. They were too far in the distance. There were no banners to identify them. They must have come from the English camp. If they bring their horses onto the bridge, I will sound the alarm. What are they doing now? I sounded the alarm.

Wallace's horse seemed to appear art my side in minutes from blowing the horn. Wallace dismounted while the beast was still moving.

"Whit's up?" he asked. I pointed to the bridge where the two knights were slowly crossing. Without a second's thought, Wallace shouted, "Come." He remounted and started off. It took me all my time to get my horse, get mounted and catch him up. "We musn't let them see our troops. They're jist here tae see whit we've goat," he shouted at me when I had eventually reached hearing distance.

By the time we got down from the hill, the two knights had crossed the bridge and were making their way along the causeway on our side. But they had not reached a point where they could see our forces. There was just the two of them and the two of us. As we neared, we could see for the first time from the emblems on their tunics that they were not English. They were Scots.

Wallace pulled up and waited for them to approach. When they did, he said nothing. The first introduced himself:

"My name is James, High Steward of Scotland."

"Aye." The monosyllabic reply was enough to elicit an introduction from the second.

"The Earl of Lennox."

"Aye. And whit might ye be wantin' tae talk tae William Wallace aboot?" It was the James who carried on the conversation.

"Ye've seen the English army."

"Aye."

"There's over six thousand spearmen and bowmen. There's over three hundred horsemen."

"Aye."

"It's a mighty force."

"A mighty force o' Englishmen that ha'e fund a Scottish voice."

"There is no need for a fight, for a battle. Many lives will be lost. We can convince the Earl of Surrey to give you safe passage."

"Whit? An English bastard will gi'e me safe passage in ma ain country, ma ain land?"

"Better safe on the land than blood on the land, and the blood of your men."

Wallace opened his mouth and gave a huge yell that echoed round the hills. "Hear that?" he said when the echo had ceased. It suddenness startled our two ambassadors. "That's a Scots voice. It wull never be heard tae speak fur the English. An' when ma Scots blood falls on Scots soil, it'll merge wi' the blood o' the mony English it took tae take me." His horse turned. I thought he was about to ride away, but he turned back.

"Go tell yer Earl o' Surrey tae fuck himself. Better, tell him tae fuck that Edward."

"And those are your last words?"

"They'll no' be if ah kin think o' a better insult."

James the Steward and the Earl of Lennox rode back across the bridge heading for the English camp. Wallace, this time intentionally, turned his horse and started back towards his camp. But he was muttering. I'm sure he was saying, "Six thoosand men an' three hunner horses. Six thousand men an' three hunner horses."

When we returned, he gave an account of the meeting to de Moray. Neither was really sure what the meeting was really about. Given both their records, they were sure an amnesty was never going to be a possibility – not that they would have contemplated it. Edward wouldn’t stand for that. Wallace still thought that the real reason was to assess the size of their force. Both were thankful that the camp was behind the hill and that there was no way it could be seen from the causeway. Their speculation ended. It was Wallace who ended the conversation:

“Prepare the men. It’ll be tomorrow.”

CHAPTER FIFTY

The Bridge

Word had been passed to the commanders and the September morning broke with the troops making their last minute preparations. Although it was just turning daylight, the priests were with them saying Mass. John Blair had managed to avoid this duty as he was on watch at the top of the hill.

We were riding round the various units checking that everything was ready. De Moray was particularly keen that each commander recognised the various horns sounds and knew how to react to them. It was when he was going through them for the second time with one commander that we were interrupted by another horn sound. This time it was the horn coming from the top of the hill. It had to be John.

Immediately we swung our horses round and were riding hard to see why he was sounding a warning horn. When we arrived, John was pointing down to the bridge. There were the first of the English horsemen crossing the bridge, two abreast.

"Here it comes," shouted Wallace, about to order the sounding of the horn. I could feel my heart pounding, just like that first time at Gargowans.

"Wait." It came from de Moray. "Wait. There's too few of them over the bridge yet. We need more than that." We waited. There must have been about thirty of them that got across.

"Now?" asked Wallace of de Moray. If anything my heart pounded louder.

"Yes, get ready to sound the horn." Then. "Wait. Look. They're turning back." And sure enough, the riders, who must have been knights from their armour, were making their way back across the bridge.

"So, what the hell wis that aboot?"

"Maybe just testing us to see our response," offered de Moray. "They'll come again."

And come again they did, after about an hour. This time only about twenty crossed before they again retreated.

"Do they no' want a fight?" It was obvious that both Wallace and de Moray were puzzled by what was going on. I was wondering how much my heart could take, one moment pounding and the next settling down. John dealt with it better. "Pish."

Then something even stranger happened. I saw movement again on the bridge. Wallace and de Moray were in some deep discussion. Probably still trying to work out what the English were up to.

"Look," I shouted. "It's two monks crossing."

"Too many bloody monks," said John.

"Aye, agreed," replied Wallace.

"At least, too many Dominicans," added the Benedictine John.

"They're Dominicans?" asked de Moray.

"Aye, bloody Black Friars. Ye want torturin' done? Just ask them."

"Come on. This might explain what's been going on," shouted de Moray. Mounting up, we rode down the hill to see what these friars, far from a populist city, wanted.

When we got down from the hill, they had left the bridge and were standing on the causeway, almost at the exact spot Wallace and I had met our fellow Scots yesterday. We didn't dismount, and, as they were on foot, it gave us a feeling of superiority.

"We come in peace," one of them said.

"Peace?" started John, but a look from Wallace told him not to finish his sentence.

"Aye, and?" asked Wallace.

"In accordance with practice," began the other, "the Earl of Surrey would like to offer you the chance of accepting the King's peace."

"Oh, aye. An' whit King would that be?" asked Wallace.

Without answering Wallace's question, he continued, "And he promises remission for your past deeds."

"Past deeds or past deids?" Wallace laughed at his own joke but nary a smile was to be seen on either of the priests' faces. They were, after all, English Black Friars and probably struggling with Scottish accents.

"We have heard your message," interjected De Moray.

"Aye, an' we would like ye tae tak' a message back tae Surrey. Tell him, we're no' here tae mak' peace. We're here tae dae battle, tae avenge oor people and tae deliver freedom tae oor country. Tell John de Warenne tae come across whenever he likes. We're aye ready. We'll meet them, even tae their beards."

He urged his horse forward a couple of steps which was quickly understood by the priests as their time for departure. They turned and started walking before turning the walk into a run and scuttling over the bridge.

"Ah think he'll get ma message. Maybe noo he'll fight," said Wallace, turning his horse and leading us back to camp. Although I was taking up the rear, and was three horse lengths behind Wallace, I could still hear him singing.

"Scotland's Freedom Bell will ring."

CHAPTER FIFTY ONE

The Battle Begins

We all stood at the top of the hill watching the English camp, but there was still no movement. It was already mid-morning and our troops had been on standby since daybreak. Emotions were taut. We were all moving from anticipation to frustration. Something had to happen.

It was de Moray who made the first move.

"Let's bring out two of the schiltrons and position them at this end of the causeway. The English'll see them. Might prompt them to react. At least our men will think we're doing something."

"Aye, let's do that," said Wallace, happy to make something happen, and ordered the appropriate horn to be sounded.

To see the troops emerging from behind the hill was a wonderful sight. They had kept their six deep formation and their tall spears were glistening in the sun. De Moray had ordered that those with the best armour be placed on the front ranks. As a result, their armour was also shining in the morning light. It was a truly wonderful sight. As I looked around, there were smiles on all our faces – de Moray, John Blair and Fraser, who had now joined us. Wallace's smile was a little different. Ours reflected our pride. His – was I reading too much into this? – seemed to suggest a knowing confidence about the outcome of the battle.

Whoever the commander down there on the ground with our troops was, he knew what he was doing. Suddenly a concerted cheer rose from the ranks. As the cheer floated up to us, Wallace's knowing smile broke into a laugh.

"Aye, we're ready fur them. Aye ready," he spluttered through his laughter.

And it was just as well. In a very short time, we began to see the English knights taking up formation on the other side of the river. We had no idea what had been going on with them over there previously – the two sorties across which had been called off, the delays as they retreated back into their camp -, but this time it looked for real, this time it looked really serious.

"This could be it," said de Moray. "Let's get the archers and horse into position."

"Aye, let's be ready for them."

"Fraser, go down and tell the archers to take up position behind and between the two schiltrons. Then get the cavalry to take up position to the west of everyone. Tell them they must not engage until we give the order." Fraser went off to carry out de Moray's orders, which were too complicated for the agreed horn sounds.

The English knights now started riding across the bridge. It would take some time for this pride of the English forces to get across as they could only manage two abreast. When they got across, the knights started to take positions on the north side of the river in an attacking formation.

"Now?" asked Wallace.

"No. Wait," came de Morays response. But the numbers were building up. True, as the line of the horse was extending, with the weight of the enormous war horses, with fully armoured knights aboard, their riders were having difficulty as the horses were sinking into the muddy swamp. It was a difficult call. Made to soon, and we would leave the rump of the English army on the south side intact, able to reform for another battle. Made to late, and they would have enough of their superior forces on our side of the river to inflict a defeat.

"Fur how long?"

To me it seemed a very apt question, for most of the horsemen were now across and what seemed like thousands of foot soldiers had started following them.

"Just wait."

And the foot soldiers began to line up behind the English cavalry.

"Maybe now. Maybe there's enough across now. Maybe we could sound the horn now," ventured de Moray.

"Sound the horn be buggered. We will lead frae the front. Come on." And he was off down the hill. Quick action by our heels and our horses were following him down at full gallop, even though the path was steep.

Wallace got himself to the front of the schiltorns. He ordered the others now to break cover and line up behind the two which had already been positioned. When he saw all the troops gathered, he shouted to them all.

"Forward. But at my speed. Dinna break ranks or ah'll break yer heads. When we move faster, stay thegither. For yer families, fur yer land, fur Scotland." And he was off. De Moray fell in beside him and John and I took up position behind. We weren't sure where Fraser was, but this wasn't the time to be worrying about such things.

We were marching towards the English.

CHAPTER FIFTY TWO

The Battle of Stirling Bridge

Riding at the front, Wallace kept the pace steady. The English troops in front were still trying to get organised. Then his sword went up and he cried, "Men, on them."

As he moved his horse to a trot, so the schiltrons broke into a run, but still keeping their shape and keeping their spears and pikes upright. Then we reached them.

I dismounted figuring that, while I had certain skills as a swordsman and as a horseman, it would be better to concentrate on one aspect of my expertise. As we were at the front, the initial fighting was hard, intense, but limited. For the most part we were disabling the horses and then trying to despatch their riders once they had fallen. At the same time, we were trying to avoid the slashing swords of these same knights.

I swung at one of the horses. Missed. But I caught the leg of his rider. Not too much damage as he was wearing chausses, mail leggings.

Shit.

But he bent down to see the damage I had inflicted. Got him in the back of the neck.

Yes.

The next horse I managed to hit just underneath his breast strap.

Yes.

I could see that one of the schiltrons was fighting its way to the end of the bridge. Their intention was to cut off the possible escape route should the enemy decide to retreat. They seemed to be making progress.

Taking my eyes off what was going on just beside me wasn't a good idea. I got kicked by an oncoming horse and its rider managed to hit me on the shoulder with the pummel of his sword.

Shit.

The fighting was ferocious. My arm was getting tired and I was beginning to gulp for air. But it was obvious we were making progress. The spears were dealing with the horses and the swords with the riders. Those knights who were on either side of the causeway could hardly manoeuvre on the boggy ground and were easily disposed of by the Scots soldiers.

A lone English archer stood before me. His six foot longbow was of little use to him at close range. My sword cut into his neck.

Yes.

The English foot were equally being dealt with. As long as the Scots kept their shape, an individual infantryman was no match for their collective spears. And as well as the pikes, most of the spearmen also carried daggers for close counter work. Those English foot trapped on the bridge were experiencing a lot of difficulty. As their colleagues tried to retreat, they were being squeezed from both sides. Those who tried to jump off the bridge, and escape by the river, were no better off. They were wearing gambesons, a quilted wool tunic, as part of their armour. As the water soaked in to the wool, the gambesons became heavier and heavier and the soldiers simply drowned.

I became involved in a sword fight with a particularly strong English knight. He was much better armed than me. He was wearing a hauberk, a coat of mail, and, even when I did strike him a glancing blow, my hits would just glance off. I was also mindful of not picking up another injury like last time. It was becoming clear he was also stronger than me. With one of his downward parries, he knocked the sword from my hand.

Shit.

As he raised his sword again to strike me, he was felled from behind by a blow from a mace. As he fell to the ground, there stood Fraser behind him, smiling.

There was chaos in the English ranks. Many were being trampled to death by their fellow men and horses. The archers hadn't had a chance to launch their lethal weapons and were now being cut to ribbons.

In an hour, it was all but over. If it had carried on much longer, I doubt if my legs would have been able to support my body. I have never felt so tired.

Afterwards Wallace reckoned that there were some five thousand English infantry dead and some three hundred English horsemen. I wasn't sure how many I had contributed, but some – some.

The battlefield looked grim. As I surveyed the scene, with a mixture of pride and pity, I couldn't help thinking that if they hadn't been English dead, they would have been Scottish dead.

Wallace, de Moray, John, Fraser and I had all got separated while dealing with our individual battles. Time to find them. After all, not a little thanks was due from me to Fraser. My guess was that they would meet up back at the top of the Abbot's Hill. I managed to find a horse, one of ours - one of the heavy English horses, of which there were a few still around, would have been unlikely to get me up the steepest parts of the hill – and rode up.

Sure enough, they were all there. I was the last to arrive. But, as I dismounted, I realised there was no sense of celebration, there was no joy of victory. And then I saw de Moray was lying on the ground being supported by Wallace. He had obviously taken a severe injury.

"Get the men tae make a carrying bed quick and get him down aff here. We'll get him attention at the camp." Then Wallace turned to him and said, "Ye'll mak it, Andrew. We've had a great victory you and I. We've still goat mair tae hiv. Ye'll mak it."

But he didn't make it. He survived for a couple of months. But then, Andrew de Moray – this tactician for Wallace, this strength for Wallace, this friend of Wallace – died of his wounds.

CHAPTER FIFTY THREE

After the Battle

But that was in the future. De Moray's stomach wound, caused by being caught by a slashing sword, was treated with a mixture of wine and oil. They thought it might have to be sewn together, but, as no-one with that skill was in the camp, messengers were sent to find someone suitable.

Even the celebrations were in the future. As the English had destroyed Stirling Bridge as they retreated, the Scots troops had to make do searching for booty among the bodies on the north side of the river. For the most part, there were meagre pickings. So some of the cavalry were given permission to chase after the retreating English. They had to wait on the tide, but were able to cross the river at Cambuskenneth and then on to Torwood, near Faukirk, where they started chasing and dealing with the English rear bit by bit. They also found that there was another force doing the same. The Earl of Lennox, whom Wallace had met on the bridge when he was with the English,had switched sides and had led a force, also to Torwood, and had started attacking the English baggage train. As was told to me, there was such amounts of booty to be had that there were no skirmishings between the two groups. They just continued to harass the departing English troops all the way across Scotland, finally giving up near Dunbar. They all felt suitably rewarded for this escapade.

We remained with Wallace. His mood varied. Initially he was fairly morose. Fraser put it down to the wounds that de Moray had suffered and how close to death his new friend was. John thought it might be seeing how many bodies were left littering the battlefield and how they were being treated by his army.

But come the next day, he was in a more celebratory mood. He met us with a flask of wine.

"So, it looks like we won," he opened the conversation.

"No' jist won," added Fraser, "crushed them."

“Aye. May the worms mak their way back tae there ain earth,” he replied, raising his flask.

This was John’s cue to produce a beaker from his person – a soldier/priest is aye ready in battle – and indicate that he might join the toast if he had some of the wine Wallace was drinking. John’s beaker was filled as others were found for the rest of us. I am not sure if it was because the wine had been taken from the English, but, before our beakers had been filled, we had John’s assessment.

“Pish.”

We talked on about the battle, about what might happen next, about what the English might do, about what we should do and about Scotland. With this victory, and the English retreating, Scotland was virtually ours. Or, at least Wallace’s. Though he was always keen to point out that we still had a King and that Balliol was still our monarch. He was less sure of how the Scottish nobles would react, though was pleased to hear that the Earl of Lennox had obviously decided to join him.

“Och, enough o’ this for noo,” he said, bringing the musings to an end. “We need tae celebrate. We need tae get the taste o’ battle oot o’ oor mouths. But first, John, prepare tae say Mass. We need tae gi’e thanks. Then we will eat and drink. And sing, Alan. We need a new sang for the night. Wan tae celebrate oor victory.”

“Yes.” It was a weak reply but all I could think of saying at the time. I could have told him that writing a new song isn’t all that easy. Or I could have offered to sing some of the songs I already knew. But I had said ‘yes’.

“We’ll a’ meet later then.” And he was off.

“Ah suppose ah’d better see aboot getting’ some altar bread,” said John. “Ye ken, it’s a funny thing this thing ca’ed Mass. Comes frae the Latin. *Ite missa est.* That means, ‘Go, it is ended’. An’ here ah am jist getting’ stertit. Some things in life jist dinna mak’ sense.” And he was off.

Fraser looked around. “Ah’m no’ sure if a’ this is ended. Ah think they’ll be back. But hell, no’ the day. See ye later, Alan.” And he was off.

I sat thinking of tunes. After all this time some of them were beginning to merge into others. Then I thought I remembered one. I started writing it down. It was good to be using the notation again.

The first and second lines were fine. The last line was fine, but the third line I was less sure of. Did it go up or down at the end. Eventually I came to the conclusion that it didn't matter. As none of the others knew the original, all that mattered was that it sounded good. That settled, it went up at the end.

Then the words. I looked across at the battle field. How could I sum all that up? What was it that made it so special? The victory, yes. So a song about Wallace? No, it should be about all who risked all. So a song about the men? Yes. But what about them? And then the obvious came to me. They were Scottish. They were Scottish men. And so I had the last line. *We are Scottish born.*

The rest took longer, but eventually it was finished, or, at least, as finished as it was going to be. I practised it a couple of times.

As freemen a' , we heard the soun',
We heard the battle horn.
The English marched on Stirling Town,
But we are Scottish born
They crossed the brig for all to see,
That dull September morn.
They knew not what their fate would be,
For we are Scottish born.

Twas English blood on Scottish land.
We heard the vict'ry horn.
They fell to ground by Scottish hand,
For we are Scottish born.

It was the best I could do in the time. It would have to do.

I needn't have worried. That night the wine and ale flowed. Stories were told. Captured booty shown. The need for a song did not seem pressing. But Wallace hadn't forgotten.

"Alan, yer sang noo."

"Now?"

"Aye, noo. Keep us frae gettin' maudlin."

I stood up and sang. And as I did, I could hear my voice getting louder. And as it got louder, I could hear it echoing from the surrounding hills. I thought it sounded.....well, good.

“Again,” came Wallace’s instruction when I finished. I started and they started joining in as best they could. And, by the time we came to the last verse, they were standing and almost shouting the last line.

Yes, it was good. Or, at least, after the copious amount of wine and of ale, it sounded good.

CHAPTER FIFTY FOUR

The Start of the Clean Up

But the new day brought with it new planning. Wallace was clear that the battle was not the end of the campaign. If he let all of the army disperse now, there would be no protection when Edward again sent his troops, as he surely would.

And in any case, there were still places in Scotland held by the English. Not least of which was Stirling Castle, which we could see from where we were standing.

"We'll tak' that castle first. Then back tae Dundee. But we dinnae need a' the men. Fraser, tell the married men that they should go home. Tell them tae take their earnings, but tell them there'll be more when we tak' Dundee. We'll a' meet up there." Fraser went off to try to organise things in the manner Wallace had instructed.

"And I'll be back for Dundee too," I said.

"Ye merrit?"

"Not exactly, but Meg and me…"

"No' exactly? Then ye can exactly stay wi' me. That's settled."

I contemplated suggesting I took John with me back to Meg so that he could conduct the appropriate ceremony, but the set of Wallace's chin would have deterred anyone from challenging him. Stay I would.

But I sent a messenger to Meg telling her that I was alive, I had no injuries and that I would return as soon as I could, but that I was needed for the time being. It sounded weak to me. I hoped Meg would hear more strength in the message.

The siege of Stirling Castle didn't last long. The English troops holding it were dispirited having watched their fellows march off in the direction of England and they obviously hadn't a lot of faith that they would return. And so it was on to Dundee.

Eventually I got a message back from Meg. It simply said, 'God keep you safe, my Alan.'

I kept thinking about that message. Why 'my Alan'? Why not 'my love'? Why no asking of me to come home? Or why not asking me when I was coming home? Just 'God keep you safe. Alan.'

But we moved on to Dundee. Yes, some of the troops came back, but not all. But, truthfully, they weren't needed. The news of what had happened at the Stirling Bridge had reached the garrison at Dundee and they had little will to fight. The castle was given up and, in its turn, it gave up an enormous amount of weaponry and treasure. Easy pickings. Where next?

And so it was on to Cupir. The castle there was still in the hands of the English. The Earl of Fife was only eight years old, so couldn't be held responsible, but the same couldn't be said for the English garrison. Some two hundred of them were slaughtered.

Others of the occupying English took the hint and departed Scotland. Just four weeks after the battle at Stirling and they were all gone. Scotland was for the Scots again.

Maybe now I could go back to Meg.

But the nobles were convening a Council in St John's Town and they summoned Wallace and de Moray. So Meg had to wait. And so it was on to St John's Town.

Wallace made arrangements for de Moray to be transported from Stirling. Walking was a problem for him and riding was out of the question, so he had the indignity of being carried on a covered wagon.

Before we arrived, Wallace wasn't sure of the purpose of the meeting. He knew the nobles were unsure of him, mainly as he wasn't one of them. But he also knew they couldn't ignore him after Stirling. He knew they were more at ease with de Moray, a fellow of noble birth. But he also knew that Andrew was struggling with his injury. The resolution of the nobles was both clever and, for them, insightful.

They made both Wallace and de Moray joint Guardians of Scotland. They would rule together in place of King Balliol.

But the celebrations to acknowledge the new status didn't last too long. Wallace had now to turn from being the conquering commander to being a ruler, as regent. No longer was it just about battles. It was about beneficiaries, about bribery, about belongings. And most of all it was about food.

The English, in their retreat, had adopted a scorched earth policy. They had burned their way south. Or , as Wallace put it, "They bastards came here an' ate oor food, then burnt what wis left when they left. Ah need tae feed the people. So……..we'll jist gang tae England an' help oorsels tae their food."

So he again summoned his army, with promises of food and much plunder, to meet outside Edinburgh at Roslin. And come they did. The troops consisted of around three thousand foot and one hundred horse. Enough. Enough to ride into England.

"Ye are soldiers," he told them, "Good soldiers. But ye are also farmers. Time tae be good farmers. Time tae help ourselves tae their harvest – the English harvest - and send it home tae oor families. They will eat this winter. And we will eat while we're doin' the gatherin'".

And so it was on to England.

CHAPTER FIFTY FIVE

To England

The feeling on crossing the border into England was a strange one.

For over a year we had been fighting to get the English invaders out of our land – Scotland. Now here we were invading their country – England. It was not something that worried Wallace.

"Did they pay us fur what they took o' ours? Then ah dinna think ah'll leave ony sillar fur them. We will help ourselves, an' feed oor ain." And off he rode. Almost to underline his lack of concern, as he was riding off, I could hear him singing: *For we are Scottish born.*

He set up camp in Rothbury, partly because it was a market town and partly because it had a ford and easy access to Hexham and Morpeth and Newcastle. He scooped up foodstuffs from the whole area without any English troops coming to stop him. Carts of food were sent back home.

Then it was on to Durham. More 'harvesting' and more carts sent to Scotland. The process meant that the army was divided up into small units which went out foraging. This made the men more difficult to control and, while they were living well off the fat of the land, it was difficult to keep discipline. An example of this was when we moved from Durham to Hexham, a distance of some thirty five miles.

On reaching Hexham Priory, John had hoped to see a thriving Augustinian community. What he and the rest of us found was a place almost in ruins and robbed of all its treasure, and no monks. We left the rest of our small troop outside and ventured in. Eventually we found three monks cowering in what was once a small chapel.

"Come oan oot," shouted Wallace. And they did. Though their demeanour suggested they were expecting a sword to sever their necks at any moment. "Where's the rest o' ye?"

"Gone," came the reply from one who had a little more courage than the other two. Wallace looked around.

"An' where's a' yer stuff? A' the precious stuff ye've been gi'en tae ease the road tae heaven?"

"Gone," came the reply from the same source. "It was taken by you Scots."

"Taken where?"

"When you find those who've taken it, they'll tell you where they've put it." The other two monks were visibly shaking now. They obviously felt that their companion had gone too far this time in his reply. There was a slight pause before Wallace shouted John forward.

"John, help them prepare fur Mass. We'll no' leave this place withoot some cleansin'."

So John scuttled off. The monks seemed relieved that this would again be a place for religion rather than execution. We watched as they set up the altar with some pieces that must have escaped unnoticed by our earlier acquisitive troops. And then, amidst all the dereliction around us, Mass was said.

We stepped outside when the service was over. John was assuring his fellow monks that no harm would come to them and that they should send messages for the others to return to this their Priory. Their looks did not suggest that they were convinced, but we bade them farewell and mounted our horses.

"Where next?" I asked. But before I could get a reply, we heard a shout. It was the monks re-emerging from the Chapel.

"They've taken it all."

"Whit?" Wallace asked.

"They've taken all the altar pieces now." Wallace looked around. It was true our escorting party was definitely smaller. The others, while we were talking outside, had gone in to the Priory, helped themselves to the last pieces of value and had ridden off. "What kind of people are you?" It was the bold one again.

Wallace didn't speak as he dismounted. I could see the whites of his knuckles as he clasped his sword, thankfully for the monks, still safely in his belt.

He sat down on a stone still without speaking.

"That stone should be by the altar." It was one of the other monks. "It's our frith stone. Anyone reaching it is guaranteed sanctuary."

"Frith?" I asked.

"It means peace," came the reply from the same source.

Then Wallace interrupted.

"So, a place o' sanctuary and safety. Bring me a pen and some vellum." John looked quizzically at him, wondering how he was going to magic such things from the thin air. He needn't have worried. While everything of value had been taken from the monks, such valueless commodities were still in their possession and pen, ink and vellum were produced.

"Ah canna replace the stuff ye hiv lost. But what ah can do is protect you and yours frae ony mair trouble frae ma men. Ah'm goin' tae write two safe conducts. Wan fur the Priory and' wan coverin' you three in particular."

They didn't seem over pleased. Whether they were less than convinced by the soon -to -be –produced safe conducts or whether they would have preferred their treasure back, I couldn't deduce. Wallace started writing. As I watched, I couldn't have been more impressed with his written words. It began:

Andrew de Moray and William Wallace.

He was still thinking of Andrew, giving him his place.

Generals of the army of the King of Scotland,

It sounded so good. It might have sounded a little pompous to the monks standing there, wondering what kind of general can't control his troops.

In the name of the illustrious Prince, the Lord John, by the grace of God, King of Scotland,

It not only sounded good, it was good. Here he was, in complete charge of Scotland and having invaded England, still giving fealty to his absent King.

With the consent of the commons of the realm,

And no mention of the nobility – 'the commons'. He still, after everything, drew his power from the common people, the common people of Scotland. *For we are Scottish born.*

He finished the writs and handed them over. He called John over. This time it wasn't a 'help them prepare for Mass', but,

“John, stay with them here. Get their place back tae normal. Let them see we ha’e some guid in oor hearts. Jine us when yer job is done. God be with ye.”

Aye, God be with you, John. It sounded good and it was good.

CHAPTER FIFTY SIX

Back to Scotland

Wallace then started balancing priorities. He had to continue sending food north. He had to instil some discipline in the troops. He had to show Edward, although still fighting his war in France, that Scotland was a nation to be reckoned with. To achieve all three, he decided to march west and take Carlisle. It was a hundred miles of marching across the hills that form the spine of England. It was November. It was cold. But it gave him the chance of an area of more food, of remaking an army from the disparate raiding parties and, of equal importance, sending a signal to Edward by capturing his most important northerly town.

It didn't all work out as planned. Yes, he managed to get his commanders to get the troops more organised. Yes, they plundered the whole area around Carlisle for food, often burning anything that was left. But Carlisle itself was a different story.

Without siege engines, they couldn't breach its defences. For a month they had the English garrison hemmed into the town, but they were making no progress. Once again the army was getting restless. He decided to head East again, taking us back across those same English hills. It was December. It was cold. It was snowing. It was freezing. It was awful.

The only bright part was that John Blair had found us. He told us his work in Hexham was done. Wallace didn't examine his assertion too closely, but both of us were wondering how he had achieved such miracles in only five weeks.

"Anyway, ye're back," Wallace offered, without over-enthusing.

"Aye. But ah was heading north, back hame," replied John.

"Naw, naw, ye'll ride wi' us."

"Ride where?" he asked. It was a good question. Wallace had been a little unclear about his new objective. The best we had managed so far was 'Durham way'.

We were camped a little outside Bowes. Although we could see the castle in the distance, it was an inhospitable place and most of us would be glad to be anywhere but here and get the snow off our feet. "Ride where?" he asked again.

"Newcastle."

"Pish."

"Come on, John," Wallace continued. "It'll be easier tae take than Carlisle. An' plenty o' takin's."

"Pish. Pish. Pish. Ah've come a' the way frae Hexham tae go tae Newcastle? Pish."

"The takin's, John, the takin's."

"The takin's nothin'. They've got a bloody wall roun' the toon. They were allowed tae tax people tae build it. Easier than Carlisle! Pish. An' that's no' all. There's mair monks there than Paris or Rome. Canny walk but fur trippin' o'er them."

Wallace started laughing and I have to admit, I joined him.

"Aye, laugh, but nae place is safe wi' so mony priests. Worse than Aberdeen. Ye've goat the White Friars – the Carmelites. Ye've goat the Austin Friars – the Augustinians. An' ye've goat the Shod Friars – the Benedictines. Too mony ah tell ye."

"The Shod Friars?" I asked.

"Aye, they cry them that fur they go roun' preachin' in sandals. No' a place fur us, William."

Whether John's own somewhat questionable religious fervour had given him the gift of prophecy or not, he was, in the end, proved accurate. Newcastle proved no place for us. It had walls, but it also had a well-organised garrison.

But worse, the weather continued to be appalling. The troops were fed up with it. They wanted home. They wanted to be back with their families in Scotland. Good defences and low morale were not conducive to victory. Wallace had no choice. He had to lead them back to Scotland.

We left as an army, but gradually it broke up as different groups began to take different routes to their homes. Some departed as friends, others departed as ones to be wary of in the future. But most departed content, with their food, with their spoils and with the knowledge that they had a new Scots leader in William Wallace.

And one more important thing happened.

The rump of the army that was with us had reached Carluke in Lanarkshire. The Scottish nobles had arranged to meet us there. Like the last time when Wallace was given the Guardianship, he didn't know the purpose of the meeting. But he did know he had to keep the nobles on side, so if they wanted a meeting, there would be a meeting and he would be there. And an important meeting it was.

They gave him the Governorship of Scotland – William Wallace, Governor of Scotland, in the name of King John, and with the consent of the community of Scotland.

And it got even better.

The Earl of Lennox, on behalf of the other nobles, knighted him. He was now Sir William Wallace. He was now one of them, a noble.

After it all, Wallace suggested to me that it was Lennox that bestowed the knighthood on him as a way of making Wallace forget the meeting on the bridge at Stirling. Mind you, Wallace was a little drunk at the time. He had been celebrating his new title.

There was just the two of us left when his celebrations became more exuberant. He started dancing and jumping around the floor, beaker in hand, trying out different ways of emphasising the word 'Sir'. Then he bade me call him 'Sir'. Then he would manufacture sentences for me to say which ended with 'Sir'. Like, 'Anything you wish me to do, Sir'. It was fun and we laugh a lot.

When he eventually slumped into a chair, he began a new game. He tried to put new words to *For we are Scottish born.* None of them worked. He couldn't fit them in to the tune. And, as his drinking continued, so his powers over the language decreased.

To help him out, I suggested *For we are* noble *born.*

"Aye, aye, ah like it. *For we are noble born.*" He sang it a few times, just the one line, to test it out. Then,

"But Ah'm no'. Ah wisnae born a noble. Ah'm a noble noo, but a wisnae born a noble. Doesnae work. Write anither sang. Ah wis born ordinary. Ah wis Scottish born." And with that, he fell asleep.

The new noble had managed already to master one of the noble arts – getting drunk. I tucked a blanket round him and started to leave. It was easy to say my unheard words.

"Good night, Sir."

CHAPTER FIFTY SEVEN

More Preparations

The next few months were largely taken up with the business of running the country. For a short time, the Governor was concerned with government.

Listening to him became part of my education. He was younger than me, but his mind was older. He concerned himself with the things of State. Like his concern with trade.

"If we canna get oor wool sold tae the low countries, then we mak' nae money. Nae money an' people are poor. If yer too poor, ye canna feed yersel' an' yer family. If yer hungry, ye canna fight. Empty bellies don't defend a nation." I remembered my voyage to the Low Countries with the accompanying wool. I also remembered the reasons for my empty belly. He talked of many other things like that. Sometimes they sounded simple, but always they seemed to make sense.

He was also concerned about keeping the country together and keeping a personal loyalty. Some of his chiefs became beneficiaries of this need as he gave them new titles. Others were simply bribed from the national purse. A select few increased their belongings by being given land which had previously been in English hands. This commander, who had become a ruler, was also becoming a politician.

But he also knew that it wouldn't be long before Edward prepared another attack on Scotland. There was no way the defeat at Stirling Bridge could be left unavenged. And no way Edward could leave a hostile nation on his borders. So the circle was completed. The politician became the commander again.

News reached us that Edward had returned from Flanders. According to our sources, he came back this March. I couldn't help but remember Andrew de Moray's words to the troops on that first meeting. Something like; 'When he's finished with the French, Edward will be back."

“Ye ken, ah kin almost here Andrew tellin’ me Edward’ll wait till the summer afore he attacks. He likes the summer fur fightin’.”

It was obvious Wallace still missed de Moray. It was only four months since he died. He missed him as a tactician, but he also missed him as a friend.

But Wallace was the sole tactician now. He moved us all down to Selkirk Forest where he again began to assemble his army. Some had been with him before, some were new recruits and some learned a new meaning for the concept of volunteering. But an army he had again and an army that needed to be trained again. He had the archers practising, he had the armourers supplying and he had the spearmen marching. But most of all, he had the spearmen with their pikes working in schiltrons. It had worked before, it would work again.

Then the regular problem Wallace had reared up again. Food. Supplying an army was never easy and food supplies in this vicinity were getting more than stretched. So where? Back to the Torwood.

“Why Torwood?” I asked.

“Alan, ah’ll gi’e ye three guid reasons. Ah ken the place. Ah ken there’ll be food aroon’ there. An’ when the English come they’ll head fur Stirling passin’ the Torwood. Is that no’ reason enough?”

“Aye, three reasons enough, William,” I answered. I knew he was right. Stirling would once again become the key. So Torwood it would be. And there was a fourth reason. It was a very large forest. A whole army could be hidden there.

But it took some time. Moving a whole army takes time and the journey was about a hundred miles. He kept the schiltrons together – there were four of them, each with two thousand men. They were followed by the archers with their longbows – about fifteen hundred of them. He told the cavalry – about five hundred knights – to follow later. It was a large exercise.

I hadn’t seen John or Fraser for a while. I couldn’t help wondering if they had made themselves scarce to avoid the jobs of ordering and provisioning they had been given for the march from Dundee. Whatever the reason, they were not to be found.

As we moved north, so Wallace had the fields we passed through destroyed. He would leave no sustenance for the English army. However right the tactics, it was heart breaking to see the devastation left behind. And worse, the looks on the faces of the farmers. This was their food, for eating or for trade. Many a stomach would go empty thanks to Wallace. It was no consolation to them that Wallace declared: "It's whit they English did when they left oor land."

It was difficult to get accurate information of what Edward was up to. Of course, we had spies and it's difficult to hide a whole army, but news always came late. It transpired that, as we were moving to Torwood, Edward was moving from Newcastle to Roxburgh. It was the summer. It was the end of June.

The news of the advancing English army swept the camp. There was a nervousness, but there was also an excitement. There was a feeling of ' bring them on', but there was also a question of how ready we were. Wallace was in no doubt as to the answer of that question.

"We're no' ready yet. The men arenae disciplined enough. Ah'm orderin' exercises every mornin'. There must be no spaces in the schiltrons or they'll break through. The formation is only as strong as each soldier in it. They've goat tae understan' that. Nae weak links."

So we prepared.

But I was so close to Meg. She was only a few miles and I could see her again. I raised the possibility with William. That he was averse to the idea couldn't have come over more strongly.

"Yer arse kin go up and doon later. Get they men organised the noo. They've goat wimen an' all."

And, as he walked away, I guessed the matter was settled. So we continued to prepare. For two weeks we worked as a unit, as a schiltron, as an army. We were getting some discipline. We were getting ready.

It was the afternoon of the 20thof July, 1298. It was a Sunday and Wallace had declared there would be no training after Mass. Most of us were lying around enjoying the summer sun. Some were sharpening their swords and pikes. Some were thinking how close Meg was. Some were stripped to the waist. Some were stripped to the waist and thinking how close Meg was. It was a quiet, sunny, Scottish summer afternoon.

The rider came into the camp at speed. He didn't wait till he found Wallace to give him the message. He shouted it out for all of us to hear.

"The English. They're here. The English. They're here."

CHAPTER FIFTY EIGHT

The Army Marches

The whole camp burst into life.

While everyone was getting prepared – this time for real -, Wallace was extracting as much information as he could from the rider. He was told that the English were camped at Listun, about ten miles from Edinburgh. It appeared that they were running out of food. Wallace tried to get an estimate of how many there were, but the answer was vague – thousands. There was also a story about ships arriving at Leith, but, to the disappointment of the English, they carried wine not food. Seemingly the Welsh troops in Edward's army did not share this disappointment and, having participated liberally in reducing the quantity of the wine, had started fighting against the English.

How much of all this was true was something Wallace had to guess. But on what little he knew, he had to make a decision. And make a decision himself without the benefit of discussing it with Andrew de Moray.

"They canna reach Stirling without ony food. They must turn back," he mused.

He instructed Fraser to take a small party to spy on the English. The main task was to ascertain how many there were and to send riders back with that information.

"He'll go back doon tae the north of England likely. Trouble is he could regroup there and come back wi' mair troops and carry mair food."

He instructed the various Scottish commanders to get their units ready to move.

"Cannae let that happen. But we canna get into battle wi' no' knowin' their numbers. Whit we could dae is creep up behind them."

He sent a second instruction to break up the camp. When we moved, we wouldn't be coming back here.

"If we cut off their baggage train, they'd be in a worse plight. Then we could make raids on the end o' their column. Jist pickin' them off."

The next instruction was that the archers should be ready to head the Scottish advance and that the cavalry should also make ready.

"Aye. That's whit we'll dae. We'll chop them off bit by bit. That way we'll never need tae stan' head tae head in battle, but we'll cut doon their numbers till we finish aff the best o' them. Aye, maybe even Edward himsel'. He'll be in no hurry to rush back."

It was on the tip of my tongue to rejoin, 'No' if he's deid', but I resisted the temptation. The instruction followed immediately. We were moving out.

But it takes some time to move an army of some nine thousand five hundred foot soldiers and five hundred cavalry. It wasn't until the next day that we actually started moving. We had to move through Torwood Forest and probably through Callendar Wood near Faukirk a distance of some five miles, depending upon which route we took towards Edinburgh.

But Wallace still needed information and none of Fraser's party had returned. He needed to know how many men constituted the English force, were they really in retreat and which way were they heading. Without de Moray's guidance, without the right kind of information, Wallace was finding it difficult to make a strategy for his attack.

He kept his troops moving throughout the day, though progress was slow. He didn't send out any scouting parties, which I felt strange. When I suggested it, all I got was:

"Yon Fraser'll tell me a' ah need tae ken." Today was not a day for long conversations.

When we reached the Callendar Wood, Wallace stopped his advancing army and instructed to set up night camp. Fires were lit, food prepared, horses fed and then the camp settled down to the usual routine of soldiers moaning. This didn't hold true for our party. A taciturn Wallace was never a good sign, so our conversation was kept to pleasantries without anyone complaining, or anyone enquiring. Oh, there were questions we wanted to ask. Like, how do you know we're going in the right direction? If we are, how long will it be before we catch up with the retreating English? And if we are going to be raiding at their tail, shouldn't we split up the schiltrons into raiding parties? And each of these questions would beget more. But we talked of the weather, what a good oak forest this was and how good the deer tasted. John managed to change the conversation by informing us that tomorrow was *The Day of the Magdelene,* remembering Mary Magdelene, and that we should celebrate Mass before we broke camp and moved on. Receiving no affirmation, he asked further:

"Is that a' right, William?" If expecting a more fulsome reply, all he got was:

"Aye." And Wallace walked off. Alone. Alone with his plans. We all hoped so.

The sun sets late in a Scottish summer and it was just beginning to set as the camp started bedding down. The moaning had stopped, the odd song had been sung and freshly sharpened weapons had been laid on the ground.

A solo horseman rode into camp at speed. As he neared, we could see it was Fraser.

"William?" he asked. He was out of breath as he asked the question but we could tell by his breathing that there was also a great sense of urgency. We pointed in the direction that Wallace had taken. Our various further questions like, you all right?, where are they?, How many of them?, were left unanswered in the air as Fraser turned his horse and followed our pointing towards the trees.

Sleep now didn't seem an option. We started discussing what the urgency behind Fraser's arrival was. We speculated on why he had returned alone. Indeed, why he had not sent one of his party instead of himself. We wondered if Edward had managed to get enough boats to Leith to take his army south by sea. Wallace hadn't thought of that one!

Fraser's horse appeared out of the wood, still being ridden by Fraser, but with Wallace on its rump, clutching with one hand onto the saddle and the other onto Fraser. He jumped down when he reached us. Quickly followed by Fraser. Even in this twilight, we could see their faces were ashen. It was Wallace who spoke:

"They're at Linlithgow. The bastards are at Linlithgow."

CHAPTER FIFTY NINE

The Lie of the Land

"Get the men awake. They'll be no sleep the night. Tell they commanders tae get ready fur a fight the morrow." And with these orders given, he sat down with us.

"Bastards. Nae food an' they're chasin' us. Linlithgow. That's whaur he had them swear allegiance tae him a couple o' years ago. By the Holy Virgin, ah don't want tae fight them here. We're ready fur open grun. What's the land like?" The question was addressed to Fraser.

"Ah rode through it, but ah canna describe it fur a battle plan. It's goat some boggy bits."

"At least at Stirlin' Brig we knew whaur the boggy bits were. Bastards." If he had been slow to converse before, now the words flew from his mouth at speed. "Find me some-one who kens the grun ower there." No-one initially moved until Fraser guessed the command was addressed to him and went off to enlist some local knowledge. "Nae food an' they're efter me? We'll need tae get oot o' this wood an' find some way of usin' the schiltrons. How mony of them are there?"

But the only person who could answer that had been sent on an errand. In the pause the unanswered question created, John asked his earlier question again.

"Will ah say Mass, William?" The ferocity in Wallace's turn suggested Blair might not live long enough to say Goodbye let alone Mass, but , after a deep breath, Wallace controlled himself.

"John, John, there's a time fur prayin' an' a time fur fightin'. This is no' a time fur prayin'. If we get through this, ah'll spend as mony hours as ye like oan ma knees wi' ye, but no' the noo. So, fuck yer Mass."

"Ah'll just say some prayers then."

"Aye, ye might get that Mary Magdelene tae pray fur us as weel."

"There's some Carmelite Friars at Linlithgow. They might be prayin' fur us too."

"An' we need a' the prayers we kin get," said Wallace. But, with less attention to God, continued, "Bastards. Ah canna believe it. They're comin' efter me. Get me some water. They bastards."

The water quickly arrived and he splashed his face. Then he turned it upward and shouted, "How mony? An' how mony horses?" He drank some of the water which had the curious effect of reducing his volume. "We've goat tae find open grun. That's whit we've trained them fur. Whaur's that Fraser? John, haud yer prayers till later. Find Fraser." And off John went, leaving just the two of us.

"Alan, this efternoon all ah could think of wis how, if we managed tae keep taking bits aff Edward's army, we could be in fur a time when he wouldnae bother us. We could've had peace in oor land. These men could've goat back tae their families. Scotland might've had the chance tae trade again. Noo it's this."

"If we win, all these things will happen."

"Win? On grun no' o' ma choosin'?"

"The men are well trained and everyone will follow you into battle. You give the orders and they will follow. Aye, to their death if necessary."

"Aye, Alan, an' it wull be necessary."

The conversation was stopped as Fraser returned with three other men. John was not with them, but that seemed to matter little. Maybe Wallace thought his prayers were over.

"These men know the land," announced Fraser.

"You come frae here?" Wallace asked.

"Aye," they replied in some form of polyphony, but the pause before their reply showed that they were in some awe, if not in some fear, in the presence of their leader.

"So, whit's it like?"

There was one, bigger than the others, who perhaps was a little less reverential and who had the temerity to ask a question.

"We a' come frae here, but what land are ye talking aboot?" the big one asked. Wallace's face coloured, but, as he had done with John, he controlled himself before he replied. He then spoke slowly.

"The English are at Linlithgow. We are here in Callendar Wood. Assuming the English head towards us," - he looked over at Fraser, then back to the men – "and assuming we move out o' this wood, what is the land like between us?"

The big one carried on.

"That way oot o' the forest, ye come tae some empty land. There's a couple o' wee rivers." But he was interrupted by the smallest of the trio.

"They're no' rivers. They're just burns." His status challenged, the big one defended himself.

"Ah said *wee* rivers."

"Ah ken ye did, but they're wee burns. One's cried the Glen Burn and the other.....has a name as weel."

Wallace picked up a stick and tried to draw patterns on the grass.

"So this is where we come oot o' the wood. This is empty grun. And here it slopes doon tae yer burns?"

"Aye," said the big one, "something like that."

"Something like that?" He took another swig of water. It had the same effect again. He spoke to them, this time, quietly. "Perhaps ah should see it fur masel'. Get them some horses. Would ye take us tae whaur yer talkin' aboot?"

"Ah canna ride," said the big one.

"Ah kin," said the wee one.

"Then you shall guide us. Ah thank ye a' fur yer help."

"Oor pleasure." It came from the third member of the assisting party, who by this stage had managed not to open his mouth.

"Fraser, you stay here and mak' sure everyone's ready tae march oot when ah get back. Alan, you come wi' me. Ah might no' be needin' a song, but ah might need the company. Right, wee man, lead us on."

"Duncan. Ma name is Duncan."

"Right, Duncan. Lead us on."

CHAPTER SIXTY

The Battle Begins

Duncan did lead us out of the wood, clearly with a knowledge of what he was doing.

When we emerged, it wasn't much different from what had been described, but seeing is different from hearing. We were on a small hill. The ground did slope away from us. The two burns could easily be seen. Between them the ground was boggy. Wallace looked around without speaking. His eyes seemed to be focussing on the distant ground. Probably trying to imagine where the English army would come from and how they might deploy. Then the Commander started talking:

"This is the best place. We'll set the four schiltrons up here with their backs tae the Wood. We'll keep them circular. We'll set the archers between each schiltron, so in three groups. We'll set the cavalry ower there, so they're ready tae come in. Aye, that bog'll be a problem fur their horses. An' by the time their foot soldiers reached us, they'll ha'e been up tae their knees in mud. Nae the best fur fightin'. This place is nae the best fur fightin' either, but it'll dae. It'll dae."

It was as if he had been talking to his other army leaders, but there was only me and Duncan and a couple of riders who were our escort behind. The best I could manage was:

"You'll tell them that when we get back?"

"Aye." And he paused. Then with a smile said, "Aye, Andrew, ah'll tell them that." I smiled back. He had discussed it with his erstwhile friend.

"An' Duncan," he said.

"Aye"

"We'll find oor own way back tae camp. You take aff tae yer family. Ye've done enough fur me."

"Thank you, sir." And Duncan started to ride off, only to be halted by another shout from Wallace.

"Oh, and Duncan. Ye can keep the horse." This time all of us were smiling.

"Thank you, Sire." And Duncan did ride off, this time uninterrupted. Wallace turned to me.

"Right. Let's get this thing organised. Back tae camp. You lead." But my sense of direction was not put to the test. Wallace spurred his horse into action and was immediately leading us through the wood at a canter, perhaps not the safest course of action with so many low-hanging branches. But arrive back at camp we did.

No sooner had he dismounted than Wallace was shouting his orders. Fraser had already got the men ready for the move, but Wallace wanted the unit commanders to know exactly the positions he had decided for them. He wanted the four schiltrons to move first, followed by the archers and finally the cavalry.

"Ah ken we'll be movin' in the dark, so take it carefully. Get everyone some food and drink noo. It'll be their last chance. Then we move. Sun comes up early an' ah want everyone in position for sunrise. And may God be with us."

So the whole army move through the night. In all there were about eight thousand spearmen making up the four schiltrons. There were about one thousand five hundred archers. There were five hundred cavalry.

When we emerged from the Wood, it was still dark, but the troops started getting into their positions. The four schiltrons were the first to take station, though when Wallace saw their arrangement he ordered that each of them move further forward. Then the archers took up their positions between the schiltorns. A cheer went up when the horsemen arrived. They positioned themselves to the north of the line. The army was ready. And ready in time as the sun was just coming up.

John Blair rode along the front of the troops blessing them. God was ready.

And Wallace looked ready. He rode down the line making sure all could see him. Then he returned and stopped in the middle. He took no water, for this time he needed his voice.

"Men, some o' ye were wi' me before. Ithers o' ye have jist jined me. Whichever, ah thank ye. But ma thanks is no' enough. Yer families thank ye, yer country thanks ye. What we will dae today is for ourselves, aye. But it's also for oor families and oor country. If we win the day, we will be free men. Free Scots. If they bastards win, they will take oor land, oor freedom and oor wimen. Is that whit ye want?"

I have never heard *'no'* being shouted in so many different ways.

"Those of you who were with me at Stirling Brig ken that we can win. Ken that we can trounce them. Ken the proceeds that can come frae winnin'. So today we will win. We must win. Each of you kens yer job. Stick tae whit ye've been telt. Nae breaks in the schiltrons. Ah said, nae breaks in the schiltrons."

This time it was *'Aye'* that echoed round in many voices.

"Ye men frae the Borders, make each arra count. Find that strength in yer right airm. We need ye today."

There was less cheering this time, but the sight of the long bows being pumped in the air, was just as convincing.

"So."

And he paused, letting all the sound die down before speaking again.

"It's your day. This is Scotland's day. I have led ye here and ah'll lead ye the day, but yer no' fightin' fur Wallace. Yer fightin fur Scotland. Yer fightin' fur yer freedom. I have brought ye tae the revel. Now...dance if ye can."

Again the cheer went up as Wallace turned his horse. And then he saw it. The sun glinting on metal in the distance. The armour on horsemen. The English.

CHAPTER SIXTY ONE

The Battle of Faukirk

The glint on the metal became a shaft of light as more and more horsemen appeared. They started riding towards us. We stood, disciplined. But as we watched, we couldn't help being a little in awe of this approaching army. The bands of colour, the power of the horses. This was the might of England.

We could see the lead horses getting caught in the bog. That's why William chose this place. We're looking down on them.

The first group have given up trying to get through the bog. They're making their way round it. At least they won't manage to pick up much speed when they try to charge uphill.

The second group is having the same problem. Can't get through the bog either. Same solution. They're going round it, only in the opposite direction. That means that they'll attack both of our outside schiltrons.

I can see the horses very clearly now. They're mighty beasts, Destriers. And their armour, the barding, steel with leather strapping. Our horses look good too, but they have many more. I guess each of these groups must have over four hundred horse.

They're climbing the hill now on either side. I'm beside Wallace. Our horses are positioned just past the last schiltron to our right.

"Stand, men, stand," shouted Wallace.

They're reaching our men now. But their horses are slowing down. These horses have no intention of being speared by the pikes. And the schiltrons are holding. Wallace's head is turning from side to side to try to see everything that's going on.

The English to our right seem to be giving up. They're backing their horses away from our men. I am looking at William to see if he is going to give the order to charge after them.

But they're regrouping. The noise around us is deafening. If Wallace is going to give an order, he'll have to do it by horn. They're setting off again. But they're not heading for the schiltron.

On the other side, the English are still not making any inroads. Our men are standing fast.

"Stand, men, stand," came the shout again.

The English to our right are attacking our own horsemen. But Wallace's attention is to the front. Two more units of English cavalry have appeared. One is about the same size as the first two groups, but the other is much bigger. And that group has riders with crossbows. There must be over two thousand English horsemen out there. I've never seen so many horsemen, presumably knights, together. This is frightening. But Wallace is back looking at the fight going on between the cavalries. I do too. But I can't make out who's winning. It's just a mass of colour and noise and glinting steel.

And to our left, the English are backing off. They haven't beaten that schiltron. These pikemen haven't moved and the horses haven't been inclined to hurt themselves.

More shouting to our right. There's horses running away, running back into the wood. It's....it's us. It's our cavalry. They're galloping off. What on earth...?

"Come back." It's Wallace. "Sound a cavalry attack," he is shouting to the lad with the horn. I can hardly hear anything. They'll never be able to hear that.

Over to our left, the English horse are coming back. But they're not going for the schiltron. They're attacking the archers in between.

"Look, William. Look over there. They're going for the Selkirk boys. They're coming in from the side," I shouted.

"The cavalry. Nae cavalry."

"You'll need to tell the schiltron to break and go for the English horse. Look. The archers are being killed."

"Nae cavalry."

And to our right, the English are regrouping. They haven't chased our horsemen. Oh, no! They're doing the same thing. They're going for our archers on that side. And the archers can hardly see them for the pikemen. This is slaughter.

"William, look at that? We must break up the pikemen."

He's not replying.

The English are withdrawing. Oh my God, the number of bodies of the archers lying there. Those left are making their way into the centre of the schiltrons. Good. There'll be some protection there.

What's going on? The English cavalry are reforming at the bottom of the hill.

"Here the bastards come." Wallace is looking behind the cavalry. Ranks and ranks of archers. I can't imagine how many. Five thousand? Six thousand? "And nae cavalry."

They're marching forward to get in range. And they've got crossbowmen too. Blessed Lady, protect us.

They're taking up position. Oh my God, the sky is raining arrows.

"William, we can't stay here. We need to move." No response. "Oh, no. William, look at our men. They're dying without fighting."

More and more arrows. How many do they have?

"William, look what's happening."

"Nae cavalry."

"But they have. Look." It's looks as though their horsemen are going to charge into the gaps in the schiltrons that the arrows have made.

William is starting to ride along our troops. What's he doing? We need to run. Our men are being killed all over the field. And the cries of the injured…

"My God. Here come the horsemen." I will catch up with Wallace. What's that noise? It's the English swordsmen, banging on their shields.

"We need to go now, William." He is looking around. The English horse are now through and decimating the schiltrons. The infantry are almost at us. They'll finish off anyone left standing.

"We need to go."

Then he shouted. "Go, men. Go. Tae the woods. Come oan, Alan. Ride. Ride as ye've never ridden before. Bastards. Retreating? Bastards."

CHAPTER SIXTY TWO

The Aftermath

And we rode. And we got away. And we escaped.

But we were the lucky ones. The English horse chased our men through the Wood and cut them to pieces. Very few managed to get away. The wounded fell prey to the foot soldiers who despatched them, sometimes quickly.

Wallace was bereft. He had fallen silent.

I pondered his words as we fled the field. 'Bastards. Retreating? Bastards.' Had he been talking about the English, or was he referring to the Scots cavalry. I didn't have the heart to ask him. Maybe I was afraid of his reply.

We were back in Torwood Forest, hiding in a hollow with branches of trees acting both as a shelter and as a way to hide us. There was just the two of us. Our horses were similarly hidden nearby, no doubt grateful of the rest after the ride we had given them.

I was trying to think again of what to say. Something that would break his silence, but something that wouldn't further upset him. Nothing came to me. Nothing seemed appropriate given the losses we had sustained. And if all his speeches had been right, where was our freedom now? What was to become of Scotland.

He interrupted both our thoughts with a quiet, "Sshh." I listened. He listened. I could see his hand slowly stretching to reach the handle of his sword. Yes, I could hear it now. There was a rustling outside. His hand now gripped his sword. His body, which had been limp in defeat, was now tense and ready to spring to our defence.

A hand appeared and started pulling our protective branches away. Whoever belonged to that hand would soon feel the steel of Wallace's sword in the belly.

"So there ye are. Pish. It's taken me hours tae find ye." It was John. John Blair.

For a moment, all the horror of the past hours was forgotten as we were reunited with our friend. Our hugging might also have been tinged with relief that it was his hand and not that of an English soldier.

"So, in Oor Lady's name, how did ye find us?" enquired Wallace, when feelings of embarrassment overtook the physicality.

"Ah kent ye wid head for Torwood. Ye must baith be covered in scratches fur a' ah needed tae dae wis follow the broken branches. Ye must ha'e been ridin' at some lick tae leave a trail like that."

"We were in a hurry," I replied, somewhat inadequately.

"Aye."

"We'd better move," said Wallace. "If a bloody priest can find us, the English might."

"They won't ken aboot Torwood. No' likely tae come this far. Probably still rakin' aboot in the bodies tae see whit they can get." It may have been true, but John knew immediately that those were not the words Wallace wanted to hear. He tried to get out of it. "Or tryin' tae find food. They must be starvin'."

"We should still move," said Wallace.

"Where'll we move to?" I asked.

"There's no *we.* John, go back. They'll no' touch you if they find ye. Do whit ye can fur the bodies. Too many tae bury, but dae whit ye can." There might have been a tear in his eye, so neither of us replied.

"Alan, ye asked before tae see that woman o' yours. Go back tae her now. Ah wish ye were tellin' her better news. Jist dinna tell her the whole truth. These are no' pictures a woman should have." We let him gently rub his eyes with the back of his hand before John answered.

"We'll dae that, William. An' you?"

"Dunno. Need tae hide fur a bit till we see whit that Edward's gonna do. Need tae meet wi' the nobles. Or at least those who havnae decided tae change sides. No' sure if some o' them hadnae made that decision a while ago."

"Aye." Now wasn't the time to discuss what had happened on the battlefield.

"Weel, eh, maybe best if we stairted?" John offered.

"Aye, ye should."

"Ye'll be a' right by yersel'?"

"Ah'll be better aff by masel. Naebudy wud imagine ah'd be travellin' alane. Ah'll keep aff the roads."

It was a strange moment. Here was the Guardian, the Governor of Scotland, talking about creeping around the countryside by himself. Yesterday he was the Commander of a great army, today he must skulk like a peasant. Hours ago he was talking of Scotland's freedom. Now he was talking of hiding from Edward. I tried the only positive thing I could think of.

"When will we meet again?"

"No' sure, Alan, no sure. Once ah ken whit's happenin' ah'll send fur ye. Now, get goin' the pair o' ye. We're no' three wimen sendin' their men tae war."

If our greeting of John was effusive, our departure from William was restrained. We shook hands. There were mumbled remarks like, *See you soon, Aye, Look efter yersel', Ah wull, God Speed, May the Blessed Lady walk wi' ye.* And John and I left him to get our horses.

"He'll be a' right. The man's an ox," said John. I wasn't sure if he said it for his own benefit or for mine.

"Let's go together," I said.

"Back tae the field?"

"Aye, back tae the field."

"Might no' be safe fur you."

"Ah'll stay in the trees if they're still around. I just want to see the place again before I go."

"That Meg's a lucky wiman."

"Why's that?"

"Yer alive, man, yer alive. Come oan. Let's go. Ah've a job tae dae. It might no' work but we'll try Absolution." Then he laughed. "By the name o' Christ, ah need some o' that as weel."

"That you do, John, that you do."

CHAPTER SIXTY THREE

Back Again

We arrived at the field. The field of blood. It was as if every blade of grass that we could see had been stained, each shining in the sun with a rusty hue instead of a vibrant green.

The English had gone, with whatever meagre pickings they had managed from our fallen fellows.

And the bodies. They were everywhere. It was impossible to count. Maybe some ten thousand of Scotland's men cut down and left. How many families, how many wives, how many children has this affected. You look around and you wonder if it was worth it. Was even freedom worth this?

John had already started going round the bodies doing whatever it was he had to do. If it is Purgatory for them, it is perhaps better than the Hell that is this field. Watching him, it is sad to see him scaring off the crows as he moves from body to body. Men who had given everything reduced to being food for the birds. A country that staked everything waiting to be pecked clean by Edward.

I couldn't wait and watch any more. I shouted over to John who stopped his priestly work and came across.

"Bad day," I said, with some mastery of the understatement.

"Aye."

"Is this it? Is it all over?"

"Aye, Alan. All over fur a lang time. Efter this, there will be little will tae fight." And, for the hundredth time, his eyes surveyed the field. "An' few men left tae fight."

"So we've lost?"

He didn't reply immediately. Then he sat down and patted the ground indicating that I should join him.

"Ken when you were back in Paris?"

"Aye."

"Pick wan o' the sangs ye learned."

"No, John. This isn't a time for singing."

"No' tae sing it. Jist think aboot it. Ye see, ye remember it. It's in yer heid an' yer heart, no' left in Paris. Ye've no' lost it. What we did wi' Wallace will stay in oor heids an'oor hearts. We huvnae lost, 'cause whit we did wis right. He wis right."

"Will we see him again?"

"Aye, but maybe no' leadin' the troops again."

"Will I see you again?"

"Aye, ye will that. Now, leave this carnage. Do whit William said. Get tae see that Meg of yours."

"Bless you, John."

"Aye, an'if there is a Guid Lord, may he bless you tae."

We shook hands, for longer than was perhaps necessary, and then I started walking back to my horse. But I was interrupted by a shout.

"And Alan."

"Aye."

"Yer still a brave little brother."

I laughed and remembered our first meeting in Dundee. Mounting my horse, I waved farewell and headed to meet Meg. It wasn't a long journey, say six miles, but it was a journey filled with differing emotions. The joyful anticipation of being with her again, the guilt that I had been spared when so many had lost their lives, the picture I hadn't to paint and a feeling of 'what do I do now'.

She must have heard horse's hooves. As I approached our little dwelling, she came running out.

Meg.

I flung myself off the horse, almost tripping in the process, and then we were in each other's arms. I had been waiting to kiss her for months, but now all I wanted to do was hold her. I didn't cry at Stirling. I didn't cry at Faukirk. But now I cried. Oh, how I cried.

Still holding me, she stroked my hair and quietly said my name, "Alan, Alan." I have no idea how long we held each other like that, but it was some time before I could gently lift her chin so that we could kiss. And we kissed. All the months of separation, all the longing that had been denied, all came out in that kiss. Only now could I speak. But I had reverted to my old laconic self.

"Meg"

"Alan."

"I've missed you."

"I know."

"Meg."

And we kissed again. This time with our bodies as well as our lips.

"Wait there," she commanded, and disappeared into our little house. Some minutes passed, but I waited. My imagination grew. She was getting ready. We were going to move from kissing to making love. This was my welcome home. Yes!

Then she came out. She was carrying……. A baby.

"Your son?"

"My son?"

"Meg," and I started hugging her again.

"Be careful. Watch the boy. He's only eight months."

"I'm a father. Meg, I love you. I love you. And I love you too,….. What's his name?"

"Alan."